SETTLE DOWN

Stephanie Perry Moore

CHEER DRAMA

Always Upbeat

Keep Jumping

Yell Out

Settle Down

Shake It

ISBN-13: 978-1-61651-887-5
ISBN-10: 1-61651-887-1
eBook: 978-1-61247-621-6

Printed in Guangzhou, China
0712/CA21201000

16 15 14 13 12 1 2 3 4 5

To Jenell Clark, Chandra Dixon, and Sarah Lundy

You all inspire me. I truly am grateful that you all are my friends. Keep on living life to the fullest. Your spunk, sass, and style motivates me to be the best me I can be and never settle for less. May every reader long to speak truth and continually strive to be awesome.

Stay amazing … I love you!

ACKNOWLEDGEMENTS

It is good to have backbone: not be pushed over and not care what others think of you. You should be a leader and not a follower. You should move to the beat of your own drum. You should walk with pep in your step.

However, being too carefree has consequences. Having a bad reputation works against you in life. Be tough, but not pigheaded. Be stern, but not rude. Be daring, but don't make dumb choices or put yourself in dangerous situations. You might feel grown, but don't rush life. Settle down and make wise choices. Bottom line: don't put yourself in compromising positions. You do have a rep to protect.

Here are massive thanks to all who help chill, think, and create.

For my parents, Dr. Franklin and Shirley Perry Sr., thanks for teaching me to settle down and enjoy every day.

For my publisher, especially Ashley Thompson, thanks for helping me settle down and make a series that can make a difference.

For my extended family: brother, Dennis Perry, mother-in-law, Ann Redding, brother-in-Christ, Jay Spencer, godmother, Marjorie Kimbrough, and goddaughter, Danielle Lynn, thanks for getting me to settle down and know family is important in life.

For my assistants: Joy Spencer and Keisha King, thanks for helping me settle down, not panic, and know I'm on point with the story.

For my friends whom I love to pieces: Leslie Perry, Lakeba Williams, Nicole Smith, Torian Colon, Loni Perriman, Kim Forest, Vickie Davis, Kim Monroe, Jamell Meeks, Michele Jenkins, Lois Barney, Perlicia Floyd, Veronica Evans, Laurie Weaver, Taiwanna Brown-Bolds, Matosha Glover, Yolanda Rodgers-Howsie, Dayna Fleming, Denise Gilmore, and Deborah Bradley, thanks for caring and getting me to settle down and appreciate the joy of meaningful relationships.

For my teens: Dustyn, Sydni, and Sheldyn, thanks for giving your mom time to settle down and write, write, write.

For my husband, Derrick, thanks for loving me so much and helping me daily to settle down and work on my craft.

For my new readers, thanks for trying my novel and settling down to get something out of the tale.

And to my Savior, thanks for blessing me and allowing me to settle down, knowing I'm right where You want me to be.

CHAPTER 1

Lower Standards

Eva, you did so good, girl," my mom cheered. We had just placed second out of eight teams in our cheerleading competition.

My father came to my other side, kissed my cheek, and said, "Yeah, Eva, you were amazing."

"Eva, you were the best!" my twin sister, Ella, screamed.

Having the three of them say something great about me at the same moment made me feel better than I had felt in a long time. See, I was known as take-no-prisoners Eva Blount, a salty, sassy, and forward junior at Lockwood High School. Everyone knew not to mess with me. I spoke my mind. I did my thing. I held my own.

At that moment, I was feeling tough, but I realized there were things in my life that truly mattered to me. One thing high on the list was my family. We had been estranged for years. Though my dad lived with us until I was five, he and my mother were never married. As a little girl, I did not know why he left us, and now that I am practically a woman, I realize he was trapped by my mom early on.

He came to Clark Atlanta University to get an education. Like most young men, he was also looking for a good time. He found that and more with my mom. She was looking for a meal ticket, and at the time he was perfect. They were both young, and the consequences of their affair were not just one baby but two. While he stuck around initially, trying to make life work, he wanted more than the projects could offer. As soon as we were not toddlers, he was out.

Like a fisherman throwing a line in the water looking for a catch, I said, "Let's all go get something to eat." They went for it. "Time to celebrate."

"Your dad probably has to get back to Samantha," my mom said, giving my dad an out.

"No, I can get something to eat. Let's do it," my dad replied, really making me happy.

Samantha was my dad's pregnant wife-to-be. Supposedly, she was more my dad's type than my mom: an educated woman with style. My mom had a little weight on her. I vowed to never let myself go like that because back in the day her body was slamming like mine. Now, while still attractive, she herself wanted to shed some pounds.

I told my folks I needed to go get my bag. My twin, Ella, came with me. We were thrilled at the thought of eating with both of our folks.

"I wanted to be out there with you guys so bad," she said.

"Please, I was just glad you were here to watch it."

"I gotta get better by regional and state," Ella declared.

I defended, "Only if you're stronger."

"I go back to the doctor on Monday," she said.

My sister gave me a hug with the arm that wasn't bandaged up. A few days back, we were at a party after a football game, and a bullet grazed her arm. As horrible as that was, she was very lucky. She instinctively pushed her boyfriend out of the way—dumbest crap in the world. Though Ella and I looked identical, we were total opposites in personality. In my opinion, she was a pushover. If she could please the world, she would.

I had backbone, and while my sister and a couple other of my close girlfriends thought they were all in love, I loved myself. I figured out a long time ago when I did not have my dad there to hold me through my nightmares that I was going to have to be there for me. Guys, in my opinion, were good for just a few things: a free meal, some quick cash, and a good feeling. They liked my body, wanted to hit it and be gone. If I liked them, two could play at that game.

Later at dinner, we were actually having a good time. Realizing that life was precious and that we were blessed to have Ella still alive softened all our hearts.

Without thinking about distractions, a distraction came. My dad's cell phone vibrated. He was so in to talking to my mom that he was not paying attention. I just picked it up and noticed it was Samantha.

"When are you coming home?" the text read.

Instinctively, I typed, "Out with my family, not sure."

Quickly she texted back, "What do you mean, your family???"

Before anyone noticed, I texted back, "Evan and our unborn child are not my only kids. I'll be there when I get there."

I smiled slyly as I erased the series of texts. I wondered how mad Samantha probably was as she read each word. She was *not* going to ruin my family dinner. Ha!

My dad could do better than Samantha. She might have a nice career and look all cute and stuff, but she was a selfish witch. My dad wanted to try to get to know us. At first I did not want to bond, but my sister did. She actually moved in with them. Samantha was threatened so much that she told my sister it would be better if she moved out, and sweet little Ella complied.

When I saw my dad touch my mom's hand, I gasped. I know it probably didn't mean anything, but it could. Samantha just had to be dealt with.

I said, "Hey, Dad, you talked about wanting to get to know me some. This weekend I know

Mom wants Ella to rest up. Maybe I could get away and come and hang out with you guys. Would that be okay?"

He turned and looked at me and said, "Eva, you want to hang out with me? Spend some time with Evan and Samantha? Really?"

The way he was saying it was like he thought I detested his other family. Actually, I did. They were a bother to me, but I had a plan.

So I put on a smiling face and said, "Yeah, I want to come."

"That would be great," he said. I could not stop smiling.

Later, he took me by my mom's to get my overnight bag. Ella looked like she did not want me to go. My mom looked like she wanted me to be tough since I was feisty, like her.

My mom hugged me tight and said, "Please, don't get into it with that lady. I know she can't push you around like she does Ella, but don't start World War III."

"I gotcha, Mom. I can handle this."

As soon as we stepped into my dad's place, Samantha looked furious. But, I knew how to play her game. The key was, I knew how to play *her*.

“Samantha, hey, thanks for letting me come over,” I crowed.

She was the one making my dad mad. Watching her frowning and rolling her eyes had me laughing on the inside. Yup, I had his wife-to-be just the way I wanted her. She made Ella look like the bad one. Now she had met her match.

While the two of them argued, my little brother tugged on my jacket. He was so cute, but he was the enemy. I could not like him. I wanted my dad back. He called me Ella.

“No, Evan, I'm Eva.”

“Ella, Ella,” he repeated.

As much as I did not want to like the little boy, hating that my dad had another kid, I was not a bad person. So I picked him up and explained that I was his other big sister. I guess I did not twirl him around the way Ella did because he looked a little disappointed. That was fine with me because I was not trying to baby-sit.

Later that evening when my dad was putting Evan to sleep, I walked in on Samantha addressing some wedding invitations. She was too happy for my taste. I was the pin ready to burst her bubble.

I startled her when I said, "You might be wasting your time doing all that. Once my dad sees who you *really* are, all this wedding planning and marriage stuff is probably going to be over."

"Why are you even here?" she stood up and said, looking like she could drop her baby any minute.

Messing with her, I re-quoted the text she thought was from my dad and said, "Evan and our unborn child are not my only kids."

"You're not planning to stay, are you?" Samantha asked, looking pretty desperate.

"If I do decide to, you're not going to run me away like you did my sister."

"I didn't mean for it—"

"You know what? Just save it," I said, cutting her off. "No need to pretend we like each other. No need to think we want the same things, and certainly no need for you to get it twisted. I am *not* Ella."

I turned and walked away with her tongue. I knew how to deal with women like her. Heck, I was *one* of them. Now that I realized I loved my dad, I was not just going to let her keep him from me. Game was on.

"Eva, you better hurry up. We're going to miss the bus," Ella said to me as if it was her job to be my mom. "Come on, girl, dang."

While I was super excited she was still alive and that the bullet only grazed her arm, there were times that the things she did just got under my skin and on my nerves. I did not operate on CP Time. I was not chronically late for everything. I was on Eva Time. What was the difference? Well, on Colored People Time you always seemed to be rushing and just could not make it there when something starts. On Eva Time you know what is up. Your intention is to make an entrance, or you just do not care about being late.

"You don't have to jump all down my throat," I said.

"I was just trying to make sure you knew what time it was. You're not even ready, and the bus could be early. You know how that lady is."

"Yup, that's why I'm not depending on her. Just take care of you, and I'll see you in school," I responded a little calmer because I did not want to fuss with my sister.

My mom worked so hard. She was already gone. My ride was coming from another person. A fine, new guy named Rico was going to pick me up. I met him at the party last week at Wax's place. Not only was Rico handsome, but he was mature. He was not young like the little high school boys at Lockwood. Rico was a man, a college dude, and maybe I was too much like my mom. Maybe there was something about college men that made me want to hook them by any means necessary.

Rico honked. I would have preferred him to come to the door. Who knows? Maybe he would have got a little surprise kiss. Though I had just met him, he seemed really cool. Even though when *I* got to college I certainly was not going to be hanging out at no high school gig, I still thought he had it going on.

"Why didn't you come inside?"

"I didn't need any moms checking me out or nothing," Rico stated, misunderstanding.

"My mom's at work."

"Oh, I can turn this car around, baby."

"No, we might as well keep on going now," I commented. It was way too fast to be expecting what I knew he was thinking.

"I got tinted windows. I was going to take you back to my place and let you see what you're in store for in a couple of years."

"Well, you were late coming to get me."

"I had to go take care of a lil' something. Plus, we're together now. Let's be adventurous," Rico said with a wink.

He parked the car in the front of the school. He leaned over and stroked my face with the back of his hand. Rico smelled so good. Then he leaned over me and reclined my seat. He took his hand and started going up my shirt.

I jerked to the side and snapped, "You can't do that."

"Why can't I? Am I being too rough?"

Then he started touching me gently. "Like that?"

"No, we're in front of my school."

"Yeah, but school's already started. I'll send you to class once I ring your bell."

His lips touched mine. He had a forcefulness that lured me in. He knew what he was doing, and he wanted me. When the actual school bell rang, I started kissing his neck, and he was moaning.

I said, "Not now, baby, another time. Let's get to know each other."

"I know you just fine," he replied. He started to handle me a little rougher.

He proceeded to enjoy himself just a little. Thankfully, there was a knock at my window. Somebody had my back. Except I was startled when I saw Dr. Sapp staring back real upset. Rico's windows were not tinted *that* much. I was caught making out in front of the school.

"Young man, do you attend Lockwood High School?" Dr. Sapp asked.

"Nah, man," Rico snarked.

"Well, then you best get to moving. Eva Blount, let's go," my principal demanded.

"I know, Dr. Sapp. I have to get to class. Can I say good-bye?"

"Nah, you got to get to my office."

"Dr. Sapp, come on," I said as he made me get out of the car and walk with him.

Rico took off. Dr. Sapp escorted me to his office. I had to sit and wait until my mom arrived. I knew she would not be happy.

"Eva, I just don't understand. Why would you make such bad decisions? This man could suspend you," my mom shouted in Dr. Sapp's office.

He and I could have talked through this. He did not have to call my mom. The way he was looking at her got me to thinking, there was more to why he phoned her to come in for a conference.

"This is just so hard. I'm doing all I can raising these two girls. It still seems like I'm not doing enough. Ella just got out of ISS, and then she ends up in the hospital. Now Eva's acting up," my mom vented.

Dr. Sapp got up from behind his desk. He came over to my mom and rubbed her back. I could not tell if she was faking it, wanting his sympathy to ease my punishment, or if I truly had upset her that much. I definitely could tell he was happy to console her. He handed her a tissue, and when I saw real tears, I felt bad. My mom was seriously going through it. Although my dad has stepped in and helped get the rent up to date, her plate was full. I was basically toppling it over with my poor choices.

"Do you have to suspend her, sir? Is there any way you can give her a warning? Eva's the last person who needs to be missing school. Plus they got this regional state cheerleading competition coming up. Can you help me out, please?" my mom pleaded.

Dr. Sapp smiled way big and said, "Yes, if you do something for me."

"Okay," my mom responded slowly.

Dr. Sapp was crossing the line. What was he talking about? And what was he insinuating? There was nothing my mom needed to do for him. I am not saying I wanted her to be single the rest of her life, but at least for now, I didn't want her to be available.

Now, Dr. Sapp was a good catch. He was an educated man bringing in big bank. He didn't appear to have baggage.

However, a part of me was selfish. My dad was already getting married. My twin sister was already goo-goo eyes over some football player on our team. I did not want to be alone. It was time for me and my mom to bond and hang out.

Being real, I could see Dr. Sapp was her type. Clean cut, slick with the tongue, and cool. He was not an uptight principal. He was checking her out way too much.

Stepping in, I said, "Uh, I'll take any punishment. My mom doesn't need to do anything for you."

"I wanted her to cook me one of those pecan pies she made last year. Don't think I forgot, Ms. Blount."

"Oh, you know I could do that," my mom laughed like a silly school girl.

"With Thanksgiving coming up and me being a single man and all, I gotta figure out how I'm going to eat. If I eat no turkey, I certainly want to have dessert."

My mom said, "Well, we can't have you alone on Thanksgiving."

"Oh no, no, no, I wouldn't dare intrude," he said, trying to pretend like he would not invite himself.

"Uh, if I'm not going to get in trouble, can I go to class?" I huffed.

"You sit on down here," my mom said boldly.

Dr. Sapp said, "Yeah, we're worried about you, Eva. If you need to talk to the counselor or anything like that—"

"My baby doesn't need to talk to the counselor," my mom interrupted Dr. Sapp.

"I'm just saying, Ms. Blount, your daughter is developing a reputation around here that I don't think you want. You told me last time when Ella was in here that you and I could talk. I'm keeping it real."

I folded my arms, pouted my lips, and looked out of his window. I did not give a darn what people thought about me. I was in front of the school making out because that was my choice. Girls wish they had it going on like I did. Guys salivated at the thought of wanting to knock my boots. I do not know what reputation he was talking about that was supposedly so bad, but I was fine with me.

I stood up and asked for a pass. They hesitated, but I stood firm so they could tell I was not shaken. When I got it, I left the two of them in Dr. Sapp's office, doing who knows what.

As I turned the corner to go to science, one of the stupid football players wasn't looking where he was going and bumped right into me. It was Landon King, the star wide receiver. On the field he was in control of his moves, but off the field ... he was a klutz. The boy tried too hard to be cool like Leo, Blake, and Waxton.

"Watch where you're going," I snapped. But then I looked at his face and saw he was real frazzled.

"Sorry, sorry," Landon responded, quickly going around me and heading into the boys restroom.

Landon had more muscles than I realized because he hurt my shoulder bumping into me. He was not even a defensive player, yet he was packing. For a fleeting second, I hoped he was cool.

Dr. Sapp walked my mom out to the hall and she yelled out, "Eva, you're not in class? Girl, you are working my nerves. The man's giving you a break, and you take your time."

I wanted to yell out, "Just get you some, Mom, so you will chill out."

But I was respectful. I smiled at them both and walked toward my classroom door. Looking back, seeing the way she was blushing at Dr. Sapp, bothered my very core. She tripped me out trying to act like she was disappointed in how I was acting, but truth be told, the fruit does not fall too far from the tree.

"School's out, so let me come and finish what we started this morning," Rico crooned.

"I can't, babe. I have cheerleading practice."

"Whatever, skip that," he commanded, immediately letting me know he really did not care about what I had going on in my life.

The last thing you could call me was an idiot. To him I was like a chicken. He liked my legs, breasts, and thighs. The thing was, I told him he had to pay to play. I needed to feel him a little. He had to have more than a cute body and a nice car to sample what I had to offer.

"Look, you gonna lose out if you don't let me come pick you up now," he threatened.

Needing the brother to chill, I brazenly said, "Well, I guess I'm going to lose out then because I don't like brothers who raise their voice at me and can't appreciate what I got going on. I don't know about those college girls who go to school with you, but I don't need to be with you every five minutes. And I certainly don't want someone smothering me."

"All right, Eva, I hear you. I like you, girl. You're feisty. I'ma have to tame you though. Them little high school boys let you run things."

“If I wanted to be with a high school boy, I’d be with one,” I uttered with confidence. “At the same time, if I wanted to be on a leash, I’d bark like a dog to your every beck and call. However, that’s just not me, Rico. So if we need to squash this and end it now …”

Wising up, he said, “I said I got you.”

“You said you got me, but then you go on and keep pressing me.”

“Nah, babe, I hear you. After cheerleading practice then, I’ll pick you up.”

“No, ugh, bye,” I groaned. I looked at the cell like there was a stupid person on the other end.

“Wait, wait, wait,” he begged before I could hang up.

“I’ve just been thinking about you, babe,” he said. “That’s all. I can’t even keep my mind on my school books. The professor is just talking, and all I’m doing is seeing images of fine Eva Blount, and now you won’t let a brother see you when he wants to. You know how to control my mind. Do your thing, and I’ll check back in with you,” he said. I guess he realized that he was ticking me off.

“Cool,” I stated.

I guess I had a thing for older men because on the way to the locker room to change for cheerleading practice, I saw a very handsome substitute teacher. He had to be in his early thirties. He had a little goatee and looked like he lifted weights. His muscles were just that defined in his shirt. I knew if Dr. Sapp saw me fawning, he would tell him it was inappropriate showing all that to us high school girls. Our math teacher was out on maternity leave, and I could not wait until the next day when I had Mrs. Byrd's class because her sub could teach me a lot.

It was interesting though. Landon seemed to be having an intense conversation with him. We all knew our real teacher left too much work for us to get done, but Landon did not need to vent to the substitute. That was twice in one day I saw him upset. The team was 7–0. What did he have to complain about?

I was trying not to do any running. We were punished if we were late and had to run laps around the gym. I looked down at my watch and saw that it was almost time for us to report to Coach Woods on the gym floor. I was actually looking forward to practice. With the momentum we had a week back, it was time to place at regional so that we could qualify for state.

When I got in the locker room, I could not wait to tell my girls about the sub whose name badge read Mr. Gunn. The five of us loved getting a laugh off of good-looking men. I liked giving the four of them a hard time: my twin sister, Ella; Charli, the captain of our cheerleading squad; Hallie, who was loud but always there to help everyone; and Randal, the shy one of our group. You never knew what Randal was thinking because she never said a word. Before I could get to them, I was shocked by what I heard.

Randal said, "So I just need you guys to give me some pointers. I mean, all of y'all have a man. Charli you're with Brenton,"

"Uh-huh," Hallie uttered sarcastically.

Ella said, "Why is that a big deal? She's with Brenton, right? Did I miss something?"

Hallie explained, "Girl, the night you got shot, Charli was all sad and crying. Well, Brenton wasn't the one who comforted her. It was Blake."

I actually saw them together myself, but I didn't pay it any attention. Charli and Hallie were real cool. Charli probably told her more than she wanted the rest of us to know. However, with Hallie's big mouth, now we all knew.

"No, it's not like that at all. I like Brenton a lot. He's my guy." Charli paused. "It's just that Blake and I have a long history and being in his arms ... Ugh, I can't explain it."

"See, that's what I'm talking about," Randal declared.

"Here you are tripping over two guys, and I can't even get one. Ella, you and I used to hang, and I couldn't even sit with you to make sure you recuperated well because every break Leo got he was trying to play doctor. I didn't think I wanted a boyfriend, but I think I do now."

Randal needed to not be so down on herself. Just as I was about to step to her and give her some advice, I was frozen in my tracks. My girl called out my name.

"Eva."

"And?" Charli interjected in a snarky tone.

"Eva has all the guys here checking her out. I'm in classes with her. Trust me, she has the boys on lock. She's so cold and mean, but they still want to carry her books. You know what I'm saying, *carry her books*. My body's not like yours,"

Randal said to my sister, alluding that my body was also tight. "But maybe I need to show off what I have just a little bit more. You know, wear more revealing clothes like Eva. The three of you guys have somebody. Eva's got a ton of choices."

"Do you think they wanna get with her? Really get with her?" Charli insinuated.

"I don't know; I'm just saying," Randal replied.

"Think revealing and all that stuff," Charli said, trying to make a point. "Ella has a man, and Eva has boys falling all over her. Which one do you want? Because if you want to know how to get a boyfriend, you need to be talking to us, not Eva."

"Yeah, somebody said she was in front of the school this morning having sex in a car and got caught by Dr. Sapp."

Hallie liked spreading gossip. I knew Charli loved getting under my skin. Hallie was her little puppet.

I had to brace myself when my sister said, "I love Eva to death—you know that—but you're right, her reputation is horrible. Sometimes people look at me, thinking I'm her. I want to go off on them and say, 'Get your head out of the gutter,' but I can't be too mad at them because Eva puts herself in those situations, thinking her body can control men. I'm just scared because one day she's gonna get with the wrong one."

"So you think my style is cool? I don't need to be more out there," Randal asked.

"No!" all three of them shouted together.

"Huh?" Randal asked.

Charli added, "Being more out there like Eva is tired. And, girl, your style is tidy and fresh. Keep it that way."

"Girl, my sister is not dirty," Ella laughed.

"I'm not saying she's dirty. That's not what I'm saying."

Ella said, "Well, what are you saying?"

"I'm saying Randal's just fine. I'm saying what we're all saying. Eva's too provocative, flaunting everything she's got in front of guys all the time. Randal will catch the right guy without lower standards."

CHAPTER 2

Relax Baby

Okay, calm down, Eva," I said to myself, truly pissed off that my sister and my girlfriends were blasting me.

They thought I was too raunchy, but that wasn't my problem. My problem was that they didn't have enough nerve to say it to my face. They waited until they were alone and turned Randal against me. With her weak little behind, whatever they said, she went for. Yeah, she should show a little bit of skin when trying to get a guy's eye to turn her way. Like any guy wants to look at somebody covered up like a nun.

I paced back and forth, wondering if I should go confront them or keep all this frustration bottled up inside. The latter was not healthy at all. We were cheerleaders together, trying to get ready for regional and state competitions. The way I felt right now, I would not flip at all. I would not hold up any stunts. I would simply let them fall.

However, there was a major glitch in my whole not-caring scenario. I wanted the trophy just as much as any of them. I had not put in all this time, tightened up my own skills, and worked hard to pull up my grades to be a detriment to the team. So I had a huge dilemma because I had too much pride in myself to let whatever mean comments they wanted to say about me slide.

I opened up the locker room door to step out and get some water, thinking that would calm me down. However, I saw my girls' guys, Leo, Amir, and Brenton, heading my way. I guess they were going to their own locker room to change.

I looked down and saw a wooden block that was keeping the door from closing completely. I probably kicked it in the way without realizing it. An idea came to my mind. I opened the door fully, put the door stopper in tightly, went over to a bench, and started undressing. If their tails thought I was fast, then whatever. I might as well clearly go for that title.

I turned my back to the door, lifted my sweatshirt over my head, and started moving my body slowly to the left and to the right. I remembered I wore my low rise briefs, and they were mad sexy. Quickly, I pulled down my jeans. When I could feel the boys breathing through the door, I took off my T-shirt only leaving me in a bra and underwear. I pretended to fall forward over the bench.

"Ouch, oh," I screamed.

I knew if I screamed loud enough, the boys and the girls would come and try to help me. When no one was picking me up, I bent down further. I looked between my legs and saw them still standing there, looking stupid.

"Help me, Leo, please," I called out helplessly.

Actually, I could have called out any of the guys' names. Maybe on the inside I was mad at my sister the most, because out of everyone, I felt she betrayed me the most. Leo quickly came to my side. When he tried to lift me up, I became dead weight so that I would fall down again.

"Oh, I'm sorry," he said, trying not to stare at my fluorescent pink bra. "Brenton, y'all help me get her up."

"Ow," I squealed, trying to make the girls head my way so that I could make my next move.

I put my arms around Leo's neck. When he tried picking me up, I pulled him down on top of me. His head landed between my bosoms and actually touched the outline of my bra.

"What's going on here?" Hallie yelled out.

Amir grabbed her when he saw she was about to go off. I knew she was not alone. Amir tried to get her out of the area, but Charli and Randal dashed over too. They were speechless when they saw Leo and me in a compromising situation. Randal's mixed-race behind was turning red. Charli looked over at her like, *See, everything we told you about her is true*.

Leo was trying desperately to get up. We were so tangled up that he could not recover before he was caught red-handed with his hand in the cookie jar. He finally helped me to my feet and rushed over to my sister. She looked devastated. I sort of felt bad, but that's what she got for siding against me.

"It's not what you think," Leo said to Ella, but she just ran away.

Charli and Randal were pissed. Coach Woods shooed the guys away. "I don't know what's going on in here. But we've got practice. All this noise and commotion, plus having guys in my locker room is intolerable."

"Talk to *her*," Charli accused, pointing at my face with her finger.

"You had better get your finger out of my face," I threatened. "Somebody needs to talk to you. Blabbing about folks when they're not around."

"What are you talking about?" Charli questioned. "You're standing here practically naked in front of your sister's boyfriend."

I lashed back, "Like you can talk! You were practically tonguing your boyfriend's cousin."

"You don't know what you're talking about," she screamed.

I was just trying to get under her skin, and it worked. All four of these girls were so sensitive. If Randal took any pointers from them, she would not be able to get a guy. They were so irritating.

"Girls, shut your mouths and hurry up and get dressed," Coach barked. "You'll be giving me laps. So snap to it."

As soon as Coach left, Charli was back at it with me. "How could you do that to your sister?"

"The only thing I was doing was getting undressed," I replied coyly. "I didn't make the guys stop and look. Guys who supposedly would never really look my way. These studs have girlfriends. Why would they be looking anyway? Besides, you can't reel in a guy with skin," I mocked.

I wanted to tell her as much as I could so that she understood I heard them talking about me. But Charli was looking down on me from so high on her horse that she did not even realize I was spitting their conversation back at them. Randal couldn't even look at me at that point. While she had merely asked them the question about whether or not she should dress like me, she did not defend me when they told her no.

"I'm gonna go find Ella," Charli said. "I can't believe what you did to her."

"And when Brenton finds out you been seeing Blake behind his back, what do you think that's gonna do to him?" I snarled at Charli.

"You don't know what you're talking about."

"Oh, c'mon, Charli. You brag too much. I heard the word."

Charli knew she could not out-talk me. She stormed off. When she left, Randal and I were standing alone.

"You heard our conversation, didn't you?" Randal asked.

"Why do you care?" I sneered. "If I *did* hear some conversation about me, you would have had my back, right? Or would I have heard you selling me out like the rest of 'em?"

"I admire you, Eva. You know you and I are tight. You know we will always stand together. With our grades, we are two peas in a pod. On the cheer squad, we stand next to each other, but when it comes to guys, they look at you. They don't look my way. The whole thing about light-skinned girls having it all is a myth. I don't think I'm ugly, but I can never get the guys like you."

The way she was talking was like she wanted me to take sympathy on her and be all sweet to her—like she wanted to cry or wanted somebody to hand her a tissue. She didn't need to sob around me, and I was not going to comfort her.

I grabbed my stuff, slammed my locker real hard, and said, "We were supposed to be two peas in a pod till you felt too embarrassed to claim me. They bashed me and you said nothing. I didn't hear you tell them how much you admired me."

"You know I'm your friend," Randal cried. "Seriously, I love you, girl."

"With friends like you, Randal, I don't need enemies." I walked off.

I knew then she was going to bawl. She was too much of a pushover. Not my problem. She had hurt me. It was time she felt the pain back.

Randal was a cute girl. I did not know why she was alone. So what, though? You did not need to have a guy to feel like you were all that. I just proved guys were not as loyal as girls thought. I went over to the water fountain to calm down. Those four chicks were not going to get the best of me. Usually, Hallie or Charli took me home, but not today. No way was I going to be accepting a ride from them. We were through.

I said nothing to my so-called friends during practice. It was funny because in warm-ups, I actually partnered with Whitney, our co-captain, who everyone thought was a snob. However, she was a better choice to be around than any of them. They all thought something was wrong with me.

Hallie came over and said, "We are going to get some food after we change up. Anywhere you wanna go?"

I looked at her, rolled my eyes, and just walked away. She had the nerve to think that I really wanted to be around them. She acted like she didn't know what was up, which I highly doubted because all of them had big mouths. I knew Randal filled them in. Randal knew something was wrong at that point.

Trying my patience, Hallie ran in front of me and said, "We need to talk, girl. We are too tight to let the group drama build. Your sister is already so upset. You just need to apologize and—"

Cutting her off, I said, "What did you just say? You know what, Hallie, get out of my face for real. You don't have to worry about taking me home."

"Well, how are you going to get home? Is it that college boy everybody saw you with? It's all around the school that you were sexing him up on the school property," Hallie scolded.

"And we know every rumor that goes around we should believe, right?" I hinted, remembering how her name was mud last year when a senior hit it and never spoke to her again. The guy lied and said how he was proud to run a train. A cat had her tongue at that point. She could not say anything because she knew how deeply she was devastated when rumors almost ruined her sophomore year. If it was not for my smart thinking—I unleashed a rumor about how he was not able to satisfy her—the jerk never would have come clean.

Couch Woods called, "Eva, you ready to go?"

Not that I wanted it to be a secret, but I hated that she yelled out my plan in front of everybody. Going home with the coach was kinda lame. It was still better than being with any of their fake behinds.

When we got in the car, I said, "Thanks so much for taking me home."

"Oh, no problem. I'm glad you asked me for a ride. I have been meaning to spend some time with you."

"You're going the wrong way," I said to her when she turned left instead of right. "Do you remember where I live?"

"Yeah, I do, but I'm not taking you home right now. I've talked to your mom, and you and I are going to go out for dinner and a movie. How does that sound?"

I just shrugged my shoulders. I did not know what she was thinking, planning, or trying, but I was ready to go home. Then it dawned on me that Ella would show up sooner or later, and the longer I was able to stay away from dealing with her, the better.

"Yeah, that sounds great," I perked up and said. "Wait, but I don't have any money."

"Oh, no, no. It's on me," Coach said gently.

"Cool. Then I'm ready to get my grub on," I teased. "Let's go."

Why she took me to see some lame animated PG movie was beyond me. There were more interesting titles out there that I wanted to see. However, it was her dime. Her restaurant choice was a little better, thankfully. She took me to Red Lobster on Candler Road. She said I could order anything off the menu.

I wanted to ask her about her family. How was her upbringing? Did she take other girls to dinner and a movie to try to get to know them? What was the purpose of all this? I honestly started to get an attitude as we just sat there, waiting on our meal.

"Look, Eva, I want to be real with you. Can we talk, like really talk?" Again, I shrugged my shoulders.

I knew I was gonna listen to whatever she had to say. It really was not a choice on my part. Why was she asking me that dumb question?

"Why do you sometimes get so angry?" she asked. "You are such a special girl. You've got spunk. You've got style. You've goy savvy. Yet you walk around with a chip on your shoulder like the world owes you something."

The anger she mentioned rose. "You don't know my life, Coach Woods."

"Well, that's what I'm trying to figure out—why are you this way? Let's talk it out."

"I don't need fixing, and I didn't ask to come to dinner. I could have done without that pitiful movie you took me to. You just wasted your money because I was asleep. If you wanna get the food to go, that's cool, and if you wanna forget dinner all together, I'm straight with that as well. People don't really do anything nice for me unless they want something, so I'm not expecting you to be any different. You ain't gonna hurt my feelings if you wanna bounce."

"Here's the thing," Coach said. "I thought you'd enjoy the movie, and I brought you to dinner because I'm having some issues with the squad, and I think you're—"

"I'm what?" I said, cutting her off. "I'm the problem."

"Well, I was going to say, I think you're the one who can fix it."

"I don't know what you mean. I don't need you to psychoanalyze me or try to get all up in my head. No need to try and get me to be on your side and stuff."

"No, you are exactly like I was when I was your age. I did not have a silver spoon in my mouth like Charli or Whitney. People around me had money, and sometimes it irked me that I didn't have any. I paid my own way through college," Coach said, showing me she could relate just as our food finally arrived.

Opening up, I said, "Okay, so you feel me. And Charli and Whitney aren't the only ones who are crazy. Most of those girls on the squad don't even understand how tough it is to struggle. We were about to get kicked out of our apartment a couple weeks ago, and because I do things that most won't so I can eat and so I can help my mom pay bills, people look at me all strange and funny. My body is the one thing I have that makes me feel good about me."

"And so what, you gonna flaunt it all over for the world to see?" Couch Woods asked.

"Yeah," I agreed. "You said you understood. You said you used to be like me. Look at you. You're a teacher making something good with your life. All hope isn't lost for me then, right?"

"No, hope isn't lost. I got myself together because I had someone who cared and helped me turn myself around."

Putting my fork down, I said, "I'm not a drunk. I'm not on drugs. And I'm not a prostitute."

"I'm not saying that you are, but your attitude sometimes can get you into so much trouble that you're getting in your own way. That's why I'm talking to you now, because I care. I don't want you to keep thinking that you can act anyway you want to. You don't have to always be so tense and think people are out to get you. Every one of those girls cares about you, especially your sister, and she came to me crying about some prank you pulled on her. And for what?"

"What? Ella went blabbing to you, and you wanna take me out for dinner to get on me? Oh, this is great. You're already on Ella's side. Everybody's always on Ella's side. She's the sweet one. I'm the mean one."

"See, that's what I'm talking about, Eva. We are in a restaurant, and you're sitting here acting like some ghetto girl. Calm down."

I shouted, "You're my coach, not my mama."

"Well, your mama said I can talk tough to you, so I am. If I didn't care about you, I wouldn't try so hard to reach you. You can't totally brush me off because you know I'm sincere. I care, even if you said that it's gonna go in one ear and out the other. You want to have an attitude; I'm going to have an attitude back. We can sit here and eat this meal in silence and not be real with each other, and you can keep on acting like a jerk and see where it gets you.

When school started, you were the first one saying Charli was feeling herself. Well, here's the thing; you're just like her."

"Whatever."

"No, the things that bother you about her are exactly how you are. She's strong-willed and so are you. You got to her and made her change, and now you need to get to yourself."

It was so hard hearing her rant about me. Who asked her anyway? I was squirming, wanting her to hush.

She continued, "Yeah, sure I can go on and let you roll your neck, let you get smart, and throw you off the team. Honestly, I could justify dismissing you because you are very disruptive. However, I believe deep down you're the same girl I was years back. As hard as you try to push everyone away, you just wanna be embraced by them. In order for that to happen, you gotta change."

It was hard hearing the words she was saying to me. One thing I did know was that she cared. Maybe I needed to take a look at what she said. I felt like life had dealt me an unfair hand. She was telling me to play that hand, and maybe

I'd see that I could win. Either way, it was my move. What was I gonna do?

"I made you dinner tonight, baby. Let me come scoop you up," Rico said to me the next night.

I had a project due for English. With all the extra practice we had been doing in cheerleading, I did not have time to play. He begged and pleaded and told me again that he had cooked for me. He wanted me to see his campus apartment. So I said yes.

Fast as he could, he said, "Cool, I'm on my way out."

This was going to be my first real date with Rico. I went and took a quick shower. I put on my best undergarments; not because he was going to get lucky, but because I wanted to feel sexy. It had been twenty-four hours since all the drama in the locker room. Once again Ella and I shared the same space, but no words were spoken. However, I needed a favor from her, so I had to be the bigger person.

"Ah, could you please tell Mom I went out?" I asked as nicely as I could, being vague on purpose.

"Where you going? It's almost ten. You probably need to run that by Mom first."

"Like I can call her on her job," I responded, knowing our mom did not like us bothering her.

Ella retorted, "You know you can call her, Eva."

"Yeah, for emergencies."

"You need to stay in without her permission. Besides, Eva, anybody who goes out after nine is looking for a booty call."

So ticked, I copped an attitude. "Whatever! That's not true."

"What else do you think a guy wants this time of night?"

"Not that I owe you an explanation, but he cooked me dinner. I might even be back before Mom gets off work." My sister turned her head and walked away. "If you don't wanna help me out, I can leave her a note," I said angrily.

Ella looked back at me and said, "Well, I suggest you get to writing."

At that point we hated each other. A car pulled up in our carport. I rushed outside.

"Dang, that was quick," I said to myself.

But I stopped short when I saw all the girls piling out of Charli's new black BMW. That girl wanted for nothing.

"Well, what are you all done up for, Eva?" Charli sniffed, eyeing my outfit.

"You better get your girl," I said to Hallie.

"You better slow your roll before you end up with something you'll regret," Charli retorted.

I certainly wanted them to be in the house before Rico showed up. But fate would have it otherwise.

Rico rolled down his window and talked in a sly tone. "Hey, girls, I got room for you too."

I could not get in his car fast enough. Whacking him upside his head was the first thing I did after shutting the door. Why did he front on me?

Rico cried out, "What? That hurt!"

"Why you flirting with my friends?"

"Dang, I was just teasing. I was saying I had enough."

"Enough what?"

"Food, dang. It's cool if you wanna keep me to yourself, baby." Rico stared at me. "Dang, girl, you look all pretty and smell all good."

He touched my leg. He was looking too much at me and not as much on the road. Quickly, I buckled up.

“Watch where you going,” I lectured.

“Can’t keep my eyes from lookin’ at what you showin’. You makin’ a brotha crazy.”

“Well, I need you to keep a sista alive. How ’bout that? I can button up.” I did.

“I like you, Eva. You so spunky. I can just only imagine.”

“Only imagine then, ’cause I told you it’s not going down tonight. If that’s what you want, you need to take me back home.”

“Why? You ain’t trying to hold out on me, are you?”

“No, I’m just trying to get to know you.”

“What you wanna know? I wanna be a rapper. I’m working on a record deal. I’ll be shooting a music video in a couple months, and the record label been casting a bunch of these college girls, but I ain’t feelin’ ’em.”

Something inside of me perked up. I was not trying to be a model, but I *was* gorgeous. So what if other people thought I showed it off too much? Why waste it?

"Maybe you can be in it with me. Your pretty self will sure sell some records," Rico purred. He cupped my chin in his hand.

Was he deliberately being stupid? Did he think I was naive? I was not one of those girls you could just say anything to. I needed proof. I would be so hyped to be on BET or MTV—like any other normal teenage girl—but I was not going to believe him just because.

"Yeah, right," I said, pulling up to his apartment.

I was impressed to see he had a two bedroom. One room was made into a makeshift recording studio. It was real bootleg, but it was enough for him to drop a few beats. He played me a little somethin' somethin', and I could not help but sway, rock, and move my hips to the beat.

"What's your name gonna be?" I asked.

"Well, you know there was a Rico Suave. I'm Rico Swagga."

"Hey," I said with excitement. We both started dancing.

"You mind if I get you on tape? I think if I show you to the record executives, they will love you. We wouldn't have to worry about a casting call, and you can have the part for real. It's paying a lil' somethin' too."

He showed me some papers that looked like a contract, but he would not let me read them. He said it was confidential. Though I had not heard of Slap Out Records, the paperwork looked official.

"I ain't gonna beg you to be in the video. It's your call," Rico said. He started to set up the camera.

"No, no, I wanna do it. It's just that I'm hungry, that's all."

No wonder I didn't see a bunch of pots and pans in the kitchen. He only had hot dogs on the stove. What spread?

"I thought you said you fixed me a meal."

"What? A brotha ain't no chef. I did cook for you."

Rico did not even give my food time to digest. Before I knew it, he had me standing up. He turned his music back on and turned on the camera. He wanted to see me work my moves.

"Nah, you too stiff. I saw you dance at the party. Don't hold back."

Trying to feel it, I said, "Perform for me.

Maybe that will loosen me up."

"Oh, you ain't said nothing bu

When he said the lyrics, I w

There was so much profanity and ne

about women. I could not imagine …hat my friends and family would say if they saw me in a video dancing to these words.

"This is not for me," I declared. I frowned and moved away.

Quickly, he said, "Wait, that's not the track we'd be using for the dancing. I just thought you wanted me to lighten the mood." Then he started singing, "I wanna get wit my girl for the first time. I wanna have the feeling that she's all mine. I want our bodies to collide on the dance floor. And shake it, take it to the bedroom for lots more. 'Cause when she gets to know all of me, there's no other place she'd rather be. Let's hit it, hit it for the first time."

As he started singing, he started taking off his shirt. Then he came over to me and start saying over and over again how beautiful I was. He went to the kitchen and came back with some wine coolers. I could tell as he lit the candle that he wanted to make the song he just sang our ality.

"You know what? I think its time for me to go now."

"You have not finished the dancing session," he commanded. Then he went over to the camera and appeared to turn it off.

"I don't think being in a video is for me."

"That's cool. Won't pressure you with dat. Why don't you just ease up some? Take a lil' sip; have a lil' nip."

"I don't want anything to drink."

"Aight, I'll take you home. Can I at least have a hug though? A kiss? Something?"

I went over to him. Instead of just a little peck I planned on giving him, he made sure his tongue slid way down my throat. He was grabbing me firmly, but I pulled back.

"Stop, I just wanted to spend time with you. I just wanted to get to know you. I just wanted to kick it for a bit."

"What? You trying to fall in love and stuff? I ain't one of them lil' high school boys at Lockwood. I'm looking for a big girl, and I thought that's what you were. You coming over to my place at ten o'clock at night, and you just wanna talk. Wassup? Let me rub on them thighs."

"You wanna rub my thigh, that's all?" I said, feeling like if I just let him do that, he would have had enough for a minute.

He smiled when I walked to him. "That's it, come here. Smile for me. That's right. Relax, baby, relax."

CHAPTER 3

Have Discretion

Relax? I am relaxed," I said to Rico. I tried to shove him away.

He pulled me back real quick. Rico started biting my neck. He got rough quickly.

"Ow," I cried.

"Come on, please," Rico said, using his hands to keep me close. "As much sass as you got, I know you like it rough."

"Like *what* rough?"

Rico shoved me down on his couch. "Quit moving around, dang. You know you want this."

He ripped open my shirt. He tore off my bra. When I tried to kick him, he punched me in the arm.

"Look, I'm not gonna fight you for what I know you want. I bring you to my place, try to make you a star, treat you all special, and you gonna give me a hard time. I thought you liked it rough, but not this rough."

As he continued having his way with me, everything became a haze. I did remember saying no repeatedly. But I was ignored. He thought only of himself, violating every part of my being.

As tears rolled down my face, I thought about my life. What had I done to deserve this? Why was he taking what I said he could not have? How come what was supposed to feel so good was so painful?

When he was done, I wanted to kill him. But I did not have a gun. I was sure he had a knife somewhere, however, so I rushed into the kitchen when he went to the bathroom. I started fumbling through drawers. I forgot about the knife when I saw a washcloth. Immediately, I turned on the faucet, not caring what temperature the water was. I started washing every inch that he touched until I realized I was in pain from the scalding water, from the assault, and from my aching soul.

"Dang, baby, I was gonna let you go in the bathroom when I was done," he noted, coming over to me and trying to kiss me.

I could not speak. I tried to say, "You bastard! I hate you. You better sleep with one eye open mother ... ugh."

I was just so overwhelmed. I could not say anything. I wanted to tell him off, but there he stood trying to cuddle me, like this was all good. Like he had given me something I wanted. Like he was my doggone boyfriend.

To make the night even stranger, his phone rang. He picked it up quickly. Then he started yelling into the receiver.

He screamed, "I told you we can't get together until one. Yes, I have someone else over here with me, like I owe your dumb self an explanation. You just be ready when I come and get you."

I looked at him with a blank stare. It all made so much sense now. You could not just go out with guys who looked all good, smelled all nice, and said the right words. Heck no. You had to know them. You had to tell someone where you were going. You had to be smart about what time you went out in the first place. My sister turned out to be right. When you went out with a guy after a certain time, chances were it was a booty call. Unfortunately, I learned the hard way that when you resist your date, you have already given him access, and when you deny him, he will stop at nothing to satisfy himself.

He saw me looking and said, "What's the problem, baby? That wasn't anybody on the phone. We just got to do a little studying, that's all. So let me get you on home so your mom don't call the police. Plus, I need to get back and get some schoolwork done. You said you had a project too, right?"

Rico was crazy, and I had no one to blame but myself. Thankfully, on the car ride home he was on his cell phone. He thought I was asleep, but my eyes were just swollen from crying. He was bragging to some guy, and I caught the jerk in a lie.

"Yeah, she bought the record-label trick. You know, you got to print me out another contract. I spilled something on this one I got. Yeah, it was good. High school meat is always fresh. Even the ones that look like they stink."

It was interesting because at that moment, when I thought I had nothing left that he could take, he grabbed the last ounce of dignity I had left when he shared with his homeboy or whoever he was talking to that basically he thought I was trash. When we pulled up to my house, he did not have to touch me, try to wake me, or tell me to get out. I opened the door, slammed it on him, and never looked back.

Charli's car was still in the carport. The girls were all working on a presentation with Ella and had gotten permission from their parents to stay late. I had to walk past them to get to the bedroom. I needed to grab my pajamas and get in the shower. My hair was mangled, my clothes were ripped, and I looked like the tramp of the night. For the first time, everything they were thinking about me I felt about myself. Coach Woods tried to tell me to slow my roll, but I would not listen. Now I was shattered. I was unable and unwilling to carry on.

"You can't say hi?" Charli called out.

Randal, having my back, said, "Leave her alone. Can't you see she's tired?"

Charli grunted. I could not be mad at her. Actually, I could not hate that Charli, Ella, and Randal were saving themselves.

While Hallie was not pure, she was not stained like me. She realized she wanted self-respect. She did not put herself out there with any Tom, Dick, or Rico. I was the only idiot of our bunch. Finally, it was like I had on glasses and could see what I had been doing to myself. For so long, I thought it was them. Them missing out on life. Them not letting their womanhood shine. Them not knowing how to truly work men with the power of seduction. Well, the joke was on me.

The shower could not get hot enough. The brand new bar of soap, which I just opened, was not big enough. My washcloth was not wide enough to help me erase it all.

There was a knock on the bathroom door. I said nothing. The knock intensified.

"Eva, it's Randal. Eva, you've been in that bathroom for a long time. Eva? Are you all right?"

"Go away," I shouted, sitting at the bottom of the tub in a fetal position while the water sprayed down on me.

"I just want to make sure you're okay, that's all," she whispered.

"It's late, Randal, please. Please, y'all go."

"We're done. We're leaving."

Then she was gone. I was relieved. I could not even muster up the strength to say thanks.

A few moments later, my sister was pounding on the door. "Eva, I need to get in there. You know this isn't fair. You've been in there for who knows how long. There won't be any hot water left for me."

I wanted to call out, "Help me, Ella! Hold me, Ella! Protect me, sis." However, all I could do was find the strength to turn off the water, dry myself off, brush my teeth, and crawl into bed. I could not let my sister know what I had done to myself. I could not tell her that she had me pegged all along.

"Why are you making all that noise, Eva? You're keeping me awake. Are you talking in your sleep over there?" Ella questioned.

The noise she heard was me crying. I could not hold back the tears. I could not close my eyes without seeing the image of Rico. Except in my thoughts, he looked different. His hands were like claws, his face was like the Incredible Hulk, and his body was hairy like a werewolf. I was distraught and destroyed.

I heard the knob turn on our bedroom door, and my mom flicked on the lights. After grumbling to herself she said, "Okay, girls, what in the world is going on in here? I come home after working all day and I'm tired. I don't feel like having to play referee between the two of you guys."

Normally, I would have defended myself and said, "Do you hear me saying anything? Although our voices sound alike to most, you know the difference, Mom. Come on, that was Ella. Get off my back."

This was not a normal circumstance. I just took it. I actually think that surprised both of them. They got wide-eyed and looked my way.

My mom said, "Eva, look at me. I know you're not asleep. I heard the two of you guys fussing."

"It was only me talking," Ella confessed.

There was my sister again, proving to be an abnormal person. She wouldn't throw me under the bus if she could take all the blame herself. And she *always* took the blame herself. When we were little, if she broke a jar, then she'd admit it. If she drank out of the milk carton, she admitted it. Every time she was caught, she did not get in trouble because our mom could not get angry with her sweet child.

I should have learned a long time ago, being honest is better than fabricating some lie. When I broke the window, I would say I did not know who did it. I got a spanking when I ate all the leftovers and did not leave Ella any. I told my mom it was friends who were over, but when I got sick from gorging on the sweet potato pie, my mom said that I got what I deserved. When I applied pressure on my sister to do something bad, I told my mom she wanted to do it, but she never believed me, and I got punished.

Yeah, I should have learned a long time ago that honesty was the only way to go. I needed my mom and sister to love me. I needed them both to embrace me. I needed them both to quit all the fussing and be there for me. I had gotten myself into some serious trouble, and the hell hole I was in, in my mind, was unbearable.

Ella said, "I was going off because she just gets on my nerves, Mom, okay?"

"Well, I need the two of you guys to fix it. I'm serious. I don't care if you have to stay up all night and still go to school in the morning.

Handle it. Y'all know I don't play that. I work too hard around here for y'all to treat each other any kind of way. Sisters, identical twins, are supposed to get along. Fix it!" she hollered before slamming the door.

"It's just not that easy," I surprised myself and muttered under my breath.

"I'm sure it's not that easy for you to tell me why you thought it was okay to show your private parts to my boyfriend. I know he's not a doggone virgin, but still, when it comes to seeing me—*us*—our identical parts—now all that's gone because you showed him. I just don't understand why you'd even do it."

She just kept going off on me, and rightfully so. I was wrong. However, I could not take it.

Very emotional, I screamed back, "I'm sorry! I was stupid, okay? Your sister is a slut. There! He still likes you, doesn't he? At least he respects you. At least he's willing to wait until you're ready. At least he didn't just take it from you."

"What? What are you saying? What are you talking about?" Ella rushed over to my bed. She stroked my forehead.

I moved to the corner of my bed. I did not want her touching me. I thought I wanted her to hold me, but I could not take it.

"Eva, please talk to me. Please tell me what's going on. Don't shut me out. Are you saying that college guy ..."

I rolled over at her empathy and nodded.

"No, Eva, no. We gotta go tell Mom," she declared, getting up.

I quickly grabbed her hand and pulled her back down. "Please, no. Nobody can know. I did this to myself."

"You didn't do anything to yourself. I know you're not trying to take the blame for this. If he raped you, then that's his fault, and he should go to jail. You can't keep quiet."

"You don't know!" I finally said. "Who's gonna believe me? All you guys thought, when y'all looked at me when I came in here, that I was nothing. You even said before I left, if you leave late at night going to a guy's house, he wants one thing. I walked around with skimpy clothes thinking I looked cute and guys just saw past the fabric. I don't know if Randal told you, but the reason I cut up with Leo is because I heard you guys talking about me. The sad part about it is y'all were right. Who would want to be like me? Who would want to end up like this? Who would want to be so broken?"

"Oh, Eva," Ella said. "I'm so sorry. I'm sorry he hurt you. You can't deal with this alone. That guy was wrong. You were always able to say stop. Student council has been passing pamphlets out about this. There will be an assembly about this topic soon. I didn't know what you were saying over there, and I'm sorry … I … Uh … I just need you to talk to Mom. Please don't make me keep this secret."

"You know our pact," I said. "When one of us comes to the other with something serious, we agreed we would keep the confidence. I need you to promise me you will do that. I'm breaking here, Ella, worse than I ever have before."

My sister tried holding me, but I did not let her. She tried again and I jerked away. She tried one more time, and I fell into her arms.

I just kept saying, "Don't tell, please, don't tell. Please, don't say anything, please."

She kissed my forehead, wiped away my tears, and said she would not. I might not have had the help I needed, but I surely had my sister's love. For now, at least I had a little more peace.

The next morning I woke up extra early. I had my mom take me to school before my sister rose. While I still needed to work on my project, I did not want to have to look at my sister, knowing she knew everything.

"You're mighty quiet this morning. You and Ella work things out?" my mom asked.

"Yes, ma'am," I responded.

"Yes, ma'am? Since when did you become so proper? Eva, talk to me. What's wrong?"

"Nothing. I'm okay," I said, trying to hold it together because I did not want to break down.

"I know it's been rough on you, me calling you out in front of the principal and all. Eva, the man could have suspended you. Besides, I don't want you to turn this all around and get mad at me and stay over there and say nothing. You know I like conversation on the ride, and you brought the tongue lashing out on yourself."

I looked down at my hands. I had acrylic nails, and two of them had broken off pretty bad. That must have happened in the struggle. One of them was so jagged it was dangerous, and if Rico were standing in front of me, I would use it to tear him up.

"I mean, Eva, as much as I'd like to think the world is fair, it's not. Women who have a reputation of being too loose have it harder in the respectable world. Do you understand what I'm saying, honey? You're just sitting over there."

I nodded. That was all I could do. I had no get up and go. My spunk was gone, and whether anyone liked it or not, I was a different person.

While in school, I was in a daze. I did not even perk up in the substitute's class. Mr. Gunn seemed nice. All the girls were making goo-goo eyes, but I was not in that number. Randal sat next to me. She kept looking my way, wondering why I had not commented on the man in charge of giving us math instruction.

When you are going through drama, you see the world from a different point of view. I could tell that Randal was sad. I called her out about not defending me. However, now my brash tactics needed to be recanted. I was too ashamed to even open my mouth. I tried as best as I could to smile her way so that she could feel better.

I was also sensitive to the girls who were not as popular, like the chick with glasses and braces who dressed like someone from forty years ago. While she seemed oblivious to the fact that her style was off, she had a melancholy air about her that longed to want to fit in.

Inwardly, I shouted, "Stay the way you are, girl. Cover up and be careful. Be happy you're in your glasses and braces. Don't flaunt too early, because if you do, you'll run the risk of getting your innocence stolen."

Time seemed to drag. I hated that I had to stay after school for cheerleading practice. I did not want to dress out; I was afraid people would see the bruises. Also, I did not want to take my clothes off. Psychologically, I was all messed up, so I asked Coach if I could sit out.

"What's wrong?" she wondered.

"Just girl stuff, Coach."

"You want to lie down in my office?"

"That would be great if you don't mind."

She looked at me as if she knew there was something else I wanted to say. My eyes were crying out for help. I did not know if she could tell that or not.

"You need an aspirin? Want me to get you some water, anything?"

I shook my head. Before she left, I got the strength to say, "You were right about everything else, Coach. I don't want you to think I didn't hear."

She came back in and said, "Oh, Eva, I've been a little on edge ever since we had that talk. I was hoping you took it the right way. I just want to help you. You've got so much potential, and I hate for unwise choices to bring harm to you, you know?"

I knew. I could not let her know how I knew, but I knew.

"Get some rest and come on out to practice when you feel better."

"Yes, ma'am," I murmured. Coach did a double take, stunned at my politeness.

What kind of person had I been? How brash and disrespectful had I been? While I felt that I could never get over what happened to me, it was also painful coming to grips with the fact that some of what I endured was actually making me better. The problem was that I was still broken.

Charli and Hallie came in Coach's office during the break. Charli said, "Look, Randal told us that you overheard us talking about you."

"She's got a big mouth," I uttered.

"And truth be told, you got a big, nasty reputation."

"That's what I'm hearing," I retorted. I really needed the two of them to leave.

I was in no mood for their lecture. What they were saying to me was not half as tough as what I was saying to myself. At least I knew my love for myself was real. I was really truly beginning to question theirs.

"Hallie, do you have anything to say to me?" I uttered. "Or do you just follow along with everything she says?"

Hallie said, "Yeah, I know people talked about me last year too, but for the record, I was never in front of the school having sex."

"Believe everything you hear and spread it around, huh?" I glared at my old buddy.

"Well, if you didn't walk around here looking like you want to gobble up every man in sight, then I wouldn't believe any ol' thing. When it barks like a dog, it ain't a fish," Hallie replied, trying to get backbone.

I did not know what Hallie was talking about, and I really did not care. "Can y'all just get out?" I begged, wanting space.

"Listen, Coach said you weren't feeling well," Charli stepped in and brashly said. "And as captain, I need you out there. So if there's any way you can save the drama for another time and get on out there so we can practice, it would be much appreciated."

"No," I snapped. I did not appreciate her tone.

Charli huffed, "No? What's wrong with you?"

"What are y'all doing here?" Ella came in and asked.

Charli explained, "Trying to get your sister to quit tripping and come on to practice. She told Coach Woods that she was tired and sick. Look at her. There's nothing wrong, and she's in no pain. She's just being lazy."

"You don't even know what you're talking about, Charli, okay?" Ella defended. "You need to get out of Eva's face, back off, and take her for her word."

"What? Don't play, Ella," Charli said.

"Do I look like I'm playing? She doesn't feel well. Leave her the heck alone. I know you're the captain, but you need to know how to motivate people the right way and not alienate them."

Charli responded, "This is already hard enough to do because we don't have you for the routine because of your injury."

"Well, Charli, it's not like Ella can help it," Hallie spoke up. "She got shot."

"Shut up, Hallie," Charli snapped.

"Wait, shut up? Who you telling to shut up?" Ella said. Then she got in Charli's face.

Charli stepped back. "Let's not turn this around. Let's not twist this around. Don't get mad at me because she's sitting over there acting like something is wrong. Ain't nothing wrong with her tail. If a guy walked in here right now, she'd get up, prance in his face, and try to get him to notice her. I'm sick of Eva thinking she's all that."

I wanted to stand to my feet, break up the tension, and just scream out loud, "No, something truly *is* wrong with me, Charli. Because I was too wild, I did learn a lesson."

But I felt too ashamed to say a word. Too beaten down to make a case for myself. No one needed to know what happened to me but my sister. I had to keep my mouth closed and have discretion.

CHAPTER 4

Inconceivable Finish

I can't believe you talked me into doing this," I said to Ella. We were junior bridesmaids for my dad and Samantha's wedding.

Over the last couple of days, since Ella stood up to Charli for me, I had been able to appreciate my sister more. I was able to open up to her and enjoy a bond that my mom always wanted us to have. She showed me she cared and was not my enemy. I liked her covering me. She was tougher than I thought.

Standing in Lakeside Baptist Church's more private sanctuary and not the big one that held three thousand people on Sunday, I knew I had to be honest. I wanted my parents back together. Since that was not happening and my dad really cared about me being involved, I had to stop being selfish. I had to help bring to life the desires of others who I cared for.

I wondered if my dad even knew the minister who was performing the ceremony. Pastor Lawrence King was almost like a god around these parts. Turn on any Christian channel and you would see him there. When you needed him to do pastor things, he was absent.

Landon King was one of the football players I was cool with. He was Pastor King's son, and everyone knew he resented his father. In a time like this, I resented Pastor Bigwig too. My dad paid a lot of tithes and was a faithful member. It was bad that when you gave so much to build the church, the pastor could not be there to help in your time of need. Guess you had the option of going to a smaller church.

I looked over at my dad; he seemed out of it. Maybe my dad was worried that his bride would drop her baby any minute. Maybe he just wasn't sure that this was the right move because he certainly was nervous. I wanted to go tug on him and say, "Hey, we can bounce. All you got to do is say the word." However, every time I mumbled, my sister hit my leg.

"Hush," Ella instructed.

"Whatever! You can stand here and look all excited, but not me," I grunted.

There were about fifty people in attendance. A bunch of my family I didn't know and family of Miss Samantha's. Boy, she got under my skin like a bad rash. Regardless of my feelings, they tied the knot.

They had a reception in one of the halls at the church after the ceremony. My mom was not there. I couldn't wait to get home and hug her. I wasn't sure she was over my dad. My parents were never married, and I was fairly certain that tying the knot was something my mom still longed for. Besides, before we left the house, she said we were beautiful, but she was not smiling when she said it.

"You okay?" my sister asked when she came back to her seat after visiting our relatives. "We got our great uncle here and some cousins. Get up and meet people, Eva."

But I didn't want to meet anybody. So what that we had relatives there? I was practically grown, and now was not a time to meet folks on my dad's side of the family. It was really sort of insulting. If they cared enough to want to meet me, where had they been all my life? I watched them with Evan, my dad's little boy. And *he* knew everybody.

Unable to stand all the happiness, I rushed to the bathroom. I didn't want to be anywhere near the bride, so I wanted to walk out when I saw her in there primping.

"Well, if it isn't Miss Eva," she taunted. In that instant she verified that all bygones were not bygones. She and I still had a fire. "I was so surprised you stood up for me at my wedding," my dad's new wife sneered.

"I stood up for my dad," I said, adding fuel.

"Ha-ha, yes, your dad. When you left my house quoting things that were in a personal text conversation between your father and me, I went and pulled his phone. I found it mysterious that I could not find the thread of communication between the two of us that I felt was out of character for him."

My eyes looked everywhere but at her. She had won. She had married my dad. Where was she going with this?

"I just came in here to use the restroom," I responded. I tried to push past her.

"No, we need to get a few things straight right now, missy."

"Missy? Who you talking to, Samantha?"

"I'm talking to you. Your dad wanted me to let it go and wanted you to stand up for us thinking that magically it was gonna make you all excited about me. Until I get you straight, you know you can't just pull any old thing on me. I come to you straight up with street talk. That's the only way I'ma get your respect."

"My *respect*? Please!" I snapped, fanning the flames between us. "So you went to my dad and asked him about the texts, and he said what? He had no idea. Why would he admit that he typed that to you?"

"Your dad would never lie to me," she responded quickly.

"Okay, so if you think I did it, why are you bringing it up to me? Perhaps it's because I wasn't the only one who saw him standing at the alter messing with his collar, like he was being choked standing there with you or something."

"What are you talking about?"

"If you checked his collar now, you will see it's loose and all wet. He was sweating profusely, probably wishing he could back out."

"He's never gonna run out on me and our children. He *married* me. He didn't shack up like he did with your mom."

If she wasn't pregnant, I swear I would have knocked her out even though I was in a holy building. Samantha did not have to go there. This was between us. My mom did not need to be dragged into it.

"When a man doesn't want to be tied down, eventually, he finds a way to undo the rope. I give him six months," I said, passing the rash on to her.

"Ugh, you make me sick," she hissed.

"Why? Because I got you figured out?" I yelled. "You're the kind of woman who's there for my dad because he has something. Let all his clients get up and walk out. He brings in no income. Would you stand by his side if he was broke? I didn't hear for better or worse in your vows. I'm only seventeen, but I know when people don't wanna say the traditional stuff it's because they've already got doubt."

"What are you talking about? Your father and I don't have any doubts."

"Nah, Evan is three, and you're about to have another baby. It's taken him, what? Four years to marry you. He wasn't dragging his feet. Except I thought the marriage came before the babies. Looks like you're not that much different from my mom after all. Like I said, I give it six months. Nah, the way my dad looked like he didn't wanna be there, I'll give it three—"

Samantha cut me off and gripped my arm. "I don't feel good."

"I'm sure you don't feel good," I sneered. I pulled away, wanting her to let go of my arm.

She clutched her stomach like a woman about to be robbed holds on to her purse. Then she grabbed the sink with both her hands. She started rocking side to side.

Fed up with her, I said, "Please, quit acting, Samantha."

"I don't feel good, okay? You're just evil. This is my wedding day. I'm standing here nine months pregnant, and you're stressing me out."

"I'm stressing *you* out? I just came in the bathroom to empty my bladder. You're the one who got all up in my face, and now you wanna talk about wanting peace and stuff."

"I am having the baby now."

"Samantha, please."

She tightened her grasp on the sink. She leaned over it like she wanted to throw up except nothing came out her mouth. A gush of something hit the floor, like someone smashed a punch bowl.

"My water just broke! I'm in labor. Go get your dad, please. Now, Eva, please!"

I ran out the bathroom and screamed, "Dad, Ella, somebody come quick. Call nine-one-one! She's having a baby!"

My father rushed into the bathroom. "Thank you, Eva. So glad that she was not in here by herself."

"Please, don't thank her. Help me! It's her fault." Samantha shot daggers of hate my way that burned my soul.

My dad looked up at me with a face that was so hurt and confused. I stepped out of the bathroom, ran down the church hall, and bumped into Landon King. He and I both looked like our worlds were shattered. There was no way his could be worse than mine. Now my dad was going to hate me. I was in a church, yet it felt like I was in hell.

Later that evening, we were at Lockwood. We were having a Saturday night football game. We were playing Langston Hughes High of Fulton County, and it was anyone's guess who was going to win.

"You okay?" Ella asked. We walked to the sidelines to get ready to cheer.

Usually we had to be there really early, but my mom talked to Coach Woods and explained we were coming from my dad's wedding. My sister looked at me, wanting an answer; in fact she knew I was not okay. She was the only one, other than Rico, who knew what I had been through. Add to that the drama with my dad and his new bride. My life was a mess. How could I be okay? Now wasn't the time or place to talk about it. I just had to get through the game and figure life out. I was tired of unraveling like a spool of thread.

It was a tight game. Defense on both sides of the ball was playing hard. While I was there,

I really did not want to be there. However, I was such a tough girl that I had to get a hold of myself. Being at a football game was not helping. There was too much noise, making my eardrums hurt. There were too many people looking at me and making me feel uncomfortable. There was too much of a responsibility as a cheerleader to smile. Smiling was the last thing I wanted to do.

The score was 14–0 at halftime. Unless we scored, our undefeated record would be gone. Blake's passes were bombs. Was he throwing to us cheerleaders? That's how far off his passes were. Then he threw the ball in Landon's direction. It was not a pretty pass either. It almost touched the ground, except Landon extended his left arm, juggled the ball, reeled it in, secured it, rolled, was not touched, got up, and ran it for a touchdown.

I was such a sports fanatic. However, everyone was screaming but me. Don't get me wrong, I was happy for our team and particularly happy for Landon. Again, I had seen and heard a few things that were tough in his life. I really wasn't paying attention to any rumors, but I knew he needed to smile.

Our guys had really come through. They scored two more touchdowns in the second half and kept our undefeated record intact. I was glad the game was over so I could go home. I couldn't jog off the field fast enough. Surprisingly, my dad was there.

"I thought Mom was coming to pick us up," I said to him.

"She is."

"Why aren't you at the hospital? The baby's okay and everything, right?"

"Thankfully, my baby's fine, but no thanks to you," he snarled like a grizzly bear at me.

"Dad, just hear me out."

"No, you need to hear *me* out, Eva. Samantha told me everything that was going on. I didn't mention anything to you about the texts. You're a teenager, and I get that I let you down in life, so I was going to look past that. But telling her I wasn't ready to get married and that our marriage would be over soon has to be dealt with. You had no right to do that, Eva. I can't believe you would say something like that. You put pressure on my wife. That was low. I just came here to tell you that you need to respect my marriage. You got that? Do you understand me?"

"If you wanna get mad at me, Dad, because I called it like I saw it, fine. If you're gonna give a reason as to why we're not gonna be cool like we haven't been for I don't know how many years, I'm down with that. I get it, but do not make me feel like all of this is my fault. If I don't know how to love, if I've been hard on people, if my tactics are too brash in life, look in the mirror!" I gave him a long, angry stare, turned, and stormed off.

That's what I get. I opened my heart to my dad, and he just took a hammer and pounded on it. I just felt like blood was gushing from my life. There was no way I could stop the bleeding.

I went into the bathroom to get some tissues. My dad wasn't the only one who needed to look in the mirror. I did have to take ownership of my own actions. I could blame him for this. I could blame him for that. But I was almost eighteen. I texted my mom to see if she was in the parking lot. I was so happy to see her text back that she was. I knew I needed to go find my sister to see if she was going home or if she was gonna hang with her friends. But as soon as I stepped out of the girls bathroom, I was met with another surprise.

"Hey, gorgeous. I couldn't wait to get to this game tonight so I could get with ya and have more fun," slimy and sleazy Rico oozed.

I couldn't believe Rico was standing in front of me. I wanted to take both of my hands, wrap them around his neck, and choke him. He needed to be gone.

"Please, get out of my way," I yelled.

He stepped in front of me and blocked my way. "Wassup? Why you tryna get away? Let's talk, baby. You know you wanna have some more fun with me."

"I don't ever wanna 'be with you' again. I said no and you took it."

"Ha, I know you ain't saying I raped you," he declared. "Girl, please, you came over to my house practically begging me."

"That's not true! Don't you lie! Don't you lie!" I screamed.

"You need to calm down. I don't want nobody thinking that I'ma monster."

"Leave me alone, Rico. Get out of my face. I'm tryna get away."

"Get away? Like I'ma hurt you? Oh, see, we need to talk about this."

"My mom is waiting for me. Don't make me scream. You see those security guards over there? I will scream." He stepped to me real close, put his hand on my shoulder, and squeezed down hard enough to make me wince.

"Let me make sure I'm really clear with you. Get this, Eva, you don't wanna mess with me. I will take you down. Right now, you need to recant this whole stupid accusation that I took it."

"I'm not taking anything back. That's what happened," I defended, not believing his threat.

"Oh, you're gonna regret that," he threatened. Like what else could he do to me?

"Are you threatening me?" I said to him, knowing he'd already taken all I had.

"Are you taking back what you said?"

"*No!*" I shoved him and ran.

I knew that he was acting weird the night we were together, like everything was great. Like that's what I wanted. Seriously, really, truthfully, did he think it was all cool? I could not believe he thought that. And to make it worse, he thought I wanted *more* foolishness. Was he crazy? Was I gonna let him get away with this? This was too much. Maybe Ella was right and I needed to tell somebody. Keeping this to myself was killing me, and I wanted to live.

All the boys were looking at cell phones, laughing, smiling, and kidding around. When I approached the bunch, guys started hitting each other. Some were looking at me strangely.

Ignoring them, I walked up to Ella and said, “Mom’s out here; I really need to go.”

“Why are you shaking?” she asked.

“It’s that guy, Rico. He’s here. He just threatened me.”

“What?”

“Don’t know why you two are all mad at *us*.” Charli was back. She came over to Ella and me. “If the shoe fits, wear it,” Charli added rudely.

“Huh? Just step away, Charli. We’re dealing with something right now,” I said.

“Oh yeah, you’re dealing with something. I can’t believe you’re showing your face around here,” Charli looked in my eyes and said.

“Just leave it alone,” Hallie said to her. “Something’s not right with this stuff.”

"It's bad, Eva," Randal commented.

At that moment, I looked at my sister. I knew it was bad that I had been raped, but why shouldn't I show my face? I didn't do anything wrong. What was Charli talking about? What had my sister told them? I was already frazzled; now, I had to deal with cheer drama. I took my sister by the hand and pulled her over to the side. I threw my hands in the air. I needed an explanation. My stance was demanding, but she looked at me dumbfounded.

"What are you looking at me weird for?" Ella asked.

"Looking at you? Please. Why are all these people looking at me? What did you tell?"

"I promise, I didn't say nothing to nobody," she answered.

"Did you say something to somebody?" I asked, thinking it might have slipped to her boyfriend and he told folks.

Just as I thought of Leo, he came out of the locker room looking for his girl. Obviously, he thought I was bullying her because he bulldozed his way between us like I was someone he needed to tackle. I knew he was already upset with me because of the weird predicament I put him in during the locker room incident. However, he didn't have to be cruel.

"Why you all up in her face, Eva? If you wanna put yourself out there, and you think that's cute and fine, that's great. But don't you know that Ella gets affected by the things you do. You guys are twins. People fretting on me like it's my girl out there like that."

"Why people fretting on you?" Ella asked. "Its okay. We are just having a little misunderstanding."

"No, I'm sick and tired of everything always being about Eva. You've got feelings in this whole thing," Leo fumed. "This is way over-the-top this time. It's not funny, and everybody on the team is laughing about it."

"See, Ella, everybody knows. Why did you tell him?" I asked my sister.

"What do you mean, why did she tell? It's out for the world to see," Charli butted in. She handed us Blake's cell phone. "Nobody said anything. This just started floating around."

"What's been floating around?" I asked.

Charli said, "Look, it's in your hand."

I looked down at the iPhone and opened up a text message that read, "Check out the biggest slut of the school." I could not believe what I was watching. There were no words, but there was a video of me dancing. Then it cut to me being forced onto the couch. The guy's back was turned the whole time, and it was just as violent looking at it as it was experiencing it.

At the end of the clip, there was a blank black screen with white words that read, "Some like it rough." I could not believe what I was reading. I could not believe what I was seeing. I could not believe what they were laughing about. All this had to do with me. Rico was serious when he threatened me. Just that quickly, he had sent some made-up video to my friends.

I wanted to pass out. I wanted to disappear. I wanted to be anywhere but in front of my peers. Why was this happening to me? Why was my life so upside down? Why were things so wrong?

"What is it?" Ella said softly.

I just handed her the phone. I started running, but I stumbled and fell. When I looked up, a bunch of football players were laughing at me. The receiver who won the game helped me up.

Landon said, "Y'all need to quit that, dang."

"No need to defend me, Landon, 'cause if you haven't seen it, you're missing a great show," I said sarcastically.

"I ain't even opened that text. What you do is your business."

I just looked at him and said, "Right."

Well, I appreciated that he was trying to make sure I had some dignity left. However, he was already making an assumption that everything he heard was accurate. I was so frustrated.

When I pushed Landon out of the way, he said, "What did I say?"

"Sit down and look at it."

I just kept on going and ran smack back into Rico. "You'll think twice next time you wanna cross me," he taunted.

"Why don't you just take a gun and shoot me? Don't graze my arm; you might as well aim for my heart."

"Your tough self, please, don't even act like this is fazing you. You're probably loving the attention. You think you're popular anyway. I just set it so every guy in this school wanna have a lil' taste like I did."

I reached my hand up to smack him, but he grabbed hard around my wrist.

"Let my daughter go!" my mom screamed.

Rico looked at her and jetted away. I fell into her arms. My heart was too weak to act strong.

"Mom, take me home."

"What is going on, Eva?"

"I don't wanna talk about it, Mom. I can't talk about it."

"You were upset when I picked you up from your dad's wedding. You're upset when I'm picking you up from a football game. Child, you are gonna have to talk to me. What is the problem?"

"I was raped, Mom, okay? There, you know it! You happy now?"

"What?!" she cried with appalled emotion. "Where? When? Who? I know I been working a lot. All I was trying to do was get you girls graduated from high school. Is it somebody we know? Do we need to go to the police? Did it happen after the game? What do we do next?"

"It wasn't today, okay? It was earlier in the week."

"Oh, baby, I'm so sorry." She wrapped her arms around me and held me tight.

People were walking by. Some were pointing and laughing.

"Can we please go home? *Please*."

"Where's Ella?"

"She's with Hallie."

"So all these people know?" my mom asked. More folks looked my way, scrutinizing me.

"The guy made some kind of recording."

"*What?* That's a crime."

"Mama, it's floating all around."

"No, seriously, that's legally wrong. That's called sexting. It's a criminal offense to send or forward things like that."

"I just want this to go away."

"If he's playing dirty like that, then he needs to go away," my mom uttered.

"Was that the guy who was just gripping your arm?" she asked. I nodded. "What grade is he in? He looks too old to be in school here."

"He's in college."

"Well, how did all this happen?"

"I went out with him when you were at work," I said quietly.

"Eva!"

"I know, Mom, I'm sorry. If you only knew how sorry I was. Every day I can't even breathe thinking about what happened. I can't get past it, and now this whole week has been the worst of my life," I sobbed. "I just wanna wake up from this nightmare and pretend it never happened, but my life keeps getting worse and worse and worse. I deserve this horrific week with an inconceivable finish."

CHAPTER 5

Very Broken

Curled up in a ball, sobbing uncontrollably, and wishing I was never born was my fate. I was okay when my mom got me home after the football game. Then she had to go into work for the night shift. As soon as I heard the door slam, my body broke out in hives, I got chills, and the pain became unbearable.

Why was this happening to me? When was the madness going to stop? How come my world was so upside down?

The front door opened again, and I grabbed the covers off of my bed, slid to the corner, and tried to hide. I could not explain it, but I was petrified. Was Rico coming for seconds? Did he tell some of his boys where I lived? Were guys coming because they wanted to try to carry out their own sick fantasies?

I just started screaming, “No, leave! Please, go! Don’t come in. Leave now. Stop!”

Without heeding my plea, I saw a shadow come into the room, but my heart did not burst as I could see it was Ella. However, my mind would not let me truly believe and comprehend that it was her. When I saw other shadows, I really got frightened.

I screamed louder than I did at any game. “Stay away! Don’t you come any closer! You guys get back! Please, get back.”

My sister walked slowly to me. “Eva, it’s me. It’s Ella.”

“Only you come, only you,” I sobbed. “Tell those boys to go, please. Ella, don’t let them touch me! Ella, help!”

Randal started crying and said, “Eva, it’s us. We’re not gonna hurt you. Please, calm down. We love you. It’s Charli, Hallie, and me. That’s it. No boys, I promise.”

“I’m going to heat up some warm milk,” Charli said. “It will soothe her.”

Charli hugged Ella before exiting the room. Hallie started pacing, and Ella continued to slowly make her way over to me.

Ella wiped my tears and said lovingly, "Sis, please calm down. I know it's been a lot. I can only imagine. You can handle this; you're tough. And we're gonna help you through it."

Charli walked in with a mug. The girls were whispering. Internally, I had a war going on. Part of me said they were the enemy. A rational part said they were who they said they were and only trying to help.

When I looked up, Ella had the mug. "Here's some milk."

I just shook my head. How could I trust them? What if there was poison mixed into the cloudy white substance?

Charli came over to me and said, "You're the toughest girl I know. You might be broken, but you can be put back together stronger and better than before. Drink this milk. Come on, girl. It's us and we love you. Drink up. Trust me."

I took the cup, but my hands were shaking. After sipping a bit of the soothing drink, I could see more clearly. They were my girls. They were here to support me. They were not leaving until I was fine. And, boy, did I need them to stay.

Finally through with every drop, I sighed, feeling much better. Charli smiled, pleased with me—and herself. She took the cup from my tight grasp. I realized how much I loved Charli's bossy ways. I leaned my head forward on Charli's shoulder and sobbed worse than I ever remembered doing ever in my life.

Thirty minutes passed before I was calmer, and I crawled back into bed. There was not a dry eye in our room. All the tissue in our place was gone. My friends cared, and that moved me.

Looking up at all of them, I said, "Maybe I can get through this with you guys in my life. With y'all standing by me, maybe I'll be okay after all. Maybe I can go on and not lose it. Thanks. Thank you so much."

"You're right. You're gonna be okay," Charli declared. She rubbed my back, clearly upset and angry. "I don't know how this guy is able to walk around free. Why don't the police have him locked up?"

"I hope he didn't post bond," Hallie said in total frustration.

"Whenever they picked him up, they needed to throw away the key," Randal replied, punching her fist into her hand.

I could not look at them. They were assuming I did the right thing and reported his behind. I knew I did not. I just wanted it all to go away. Charli could pick up on my uneasy mannerisms.

As gently as she could, she asked, "Eva, please tell me you reported this."

"I … I …," I stuttered, but more words would not come.

"Talk to me, Eva. You of all people should not be scared," Charli grabbed my hand and demanded boldly.

"Leave her alone, Charli," Ella defended. "You guys just back up. Give her some space so she can calm down. Y'all didn't see how broke down she was after y'all left that night.

My sister pulled the three of them away from me. I could see in Charli, Hallie, and Randal's eyes that they were all dumbfounded that I kept this information to myself. I hated that I let them down. I hated even worse that I let a rapist go free. However, it wasn't as simple as they thought. My world was shattered since this happened and lucid thought was not easy to come by.

"Oh my gosh!" Randal cried out in shock. "This happened the night we were here working on the project, didn't it? No wonder you looked so disoriented, and you were in the bathroom forever."

Needing them to understand, I opened up and said, "Yeah, I was trying to scrub everything off of me. I should have, *truly should have*, gone to the police. I know it. Seeing him causing more damage makes me sick, but I just wanted this all to go away."

"The only way to make sure that this truly goes away—" Charli commented, trying to step around Ella.

Ella stood her ground. "No, Charli, you've said enough. She doesn't want to say anything. Can't you see this is hard on her?"

"It's okay," I sighed. I reached out my hand, longing for Charli's touch to give me strength.

Charli took my hand and said, "I feel for you. I hate what you're going through. I'm not trying to say it will be easy to stand up, but you have to because that guy could do this to somebody else. The problem is the video he's forwarding to people makes it look like you consented."

I shouted, "No, that's not how it happened. I thought only part of it was being taped. He told me I was auditioning for a music video. I asked for proof that he had a record deal. He showed me a contract, so I said I'd dance for the camera. Then I heard the song and wanted out. Out of dancing. Out of his place. When he came on to me, I was out of his grip. The video makes it look like I was for it, but I was saying no over and over again."

"Then let's go. Let's go to the cops right now," Charli begged, trying to get me out of bed.

Pulling my hand away, I sat flat on the bed and said, "Go to the cops? For what? Weren't you here that night? I went to the bathroom and washed away everything."

Charli continued, "Yeah, but we can testify. You came here and your clothes were torn. You appeared to be in a trance—"

"But I didn't say to any of you guys that I was raped, did I?" I explained.

Charli, being Charli said, "Cops don't care about that stuff. They wanna get the bad guys, and what this guy did to you … you got to stand."

I put my knees to my face, buried my head forward, and just started rocking again. Was Charli right? Would the police care? No way, I thought.

Venting, I looked up and uttered, "It's not gonna make a difference. It's not gonna matter. You guys—my best friends—thought I was a slut. I wasn't a virgin. I brought this on me."

"No," my sister said. "You didn't. If you said no, then he was supposed to stop. We can see that this has made you feel worthless. To help you feel strong again, we should definitely fight this and show that son of a—"

"Okay, okay," Randal said to Ella. "Let's all stay cool and not let this guy and what he did get to us. This whole thing can make us stronger."

"Yeah, let's let this make us stronger," Hallie agreed. "Eva, we are here with you and for you. You want to report this? Let's do it together."

It was 11:30 p.m. when my friends and sister wanted to take me downtown to APD to report this crime. I was angry. I was bitter. I was shattered. However, I did have a duty to at least try and protect the next girl Rico might prey upon.

So borrowing their strength that I usually never needed because I had so much of my own, I got up, put on my clothes, looked at the four of them, and said, "I'm ready."

"You sure?" Ella asked, making sure I wanted this.

"She's sure," Charli replied. She was just happy I agreed, for whatever reason.

And with that, the five of us walked out the door. Our mission was to break Rico as he had broken me. As Hallie had promised, we were on that mission together.

"Okay, this is the police station," Hallie said. We pulled up to the eerie place in downtown Atlanta in Hallie's junky car. This was no place for Charli's BMW. "This is it, Eva."

"I don't want to go in there by myself," I said to my friends.

"It's late, you guys. We should just stay together," Ella said. So we all stayed in the car as Hallie drove around back to park.

As we walked up, I got all kinds of knots and twists in my stomach, and I realized I was never going to pick on my sister again. Being the tough one for so long, I could never relate to why she got nervous or uneasy. I never felt weird, but now I clearly got it. Some things were just too much to bear, and while I had a great capacity to be able to overcome the mishaps of life, I had finally reached a breaking point.

There were two young cops at the desk. When they saw the five of us coming, they started smiling too wide. That reaction was one I usually used to my advantage. I understood that guys liked to flirt, and flirting back to get my way was my thing. Now, I was past all that. I understood that my body was more than an object. I was to be respected, appreciated, and taken seriously. It was time for business, not time for them to get their kicks. Though it was late, they were on duty, and I was not going to tolerate being mistreated.

"Well, well, well, Officer Brown, what do we have here?" the fatter guy called out to his buddy. His name badge said Officer Walker.

The taller and more underfed-looking one said, "I don't know, Officer Walker. I'd say these five pretty young ladies are probably coming in here to report their cat missing."

I could tell Charli was insulted. She rolled her eyes and looked at me like we needed to jump them. If they hadn't been cops, I would have decked them both.

Instead, the lady in her tried the sweet approach as she stepped to the two of them and said, "We need to talk to a special victims detective, and we'd appreciate professionalism."

Officer Walker was short and wide. He looked at Charli and said, "Are you insinuating—"

"I'm just saying, sir, a cat? I just told you what we're here for. This is serious. Can you get us somebody to talk to?" Charli said without flinching.

"Hold up now, missy," Officer Walker said. He shook his finger at us like we were kids. "We got to take down some information, and just because you watch *Law and Order* doesn't mean you get to come in here and try to tell us how to do our jobs."

"No, I demand to speak to your superiors so I can tell them that you are not doing your job," Charli shot back, probably wanting to tell them her dad was a state court judge, and he had friends who could get them gone.

"This wasn't a good idea," I leaned over and whispered to Ella.

Ella took her hand and bounced it up and down as if she was dribbling a basketball. "Let Charli handle it. Some guys are jerks. It's fine. This is important. We'll get to the good cops."

About ten minutes later, an older African American gentlemen came up to the front and in an irritated tone barked, "I'm Officer Crowell. Who is making the claim?"

None of us moved. The gruff officer with a belly like Santa Claus intimidated us more than the two jokers at the front desk. I sucked in my breath. There was no way, I thought, that this irritated old cop would care anything about what had happened to me.

"We all want to go back there, sir," Charli verbalized, not wanting to let me go alone.

Officer Crowell squinted and scoffed our way, clearly not liking that his question wasn't answered. "I only need to see the person making the claim. Now, unless all of you guys were violated, you'll have to remain here."

The four of them were putting up a fight with the officer. The Saint Nick impersonator was getting fed up. The front desk officers looked at him like we were a handful.

Finally, I stood up and said, "It's me. I'm the one."

"Okay, right this way." Officer Crowell exhaled. He was clearly tired of our antics.

"If you need us, you call us," Charli stressed.

"I love you," Ella said when I passed her.

"Don't hold back anything. Tell it all," Hallie advised with a supportive wink.

"I know it's hard," Randal told me. "But you can do it."

I know every officer, just like every person, has different ways. Officer Crowell was one I should be able to relate to because he was like me, straight to the point. He was not trying to make conversation. He was not trying to be my friend. He was not even trying to calm me. He just wanted facts. However, I needed compassion, and he was not the person to give it to me.

"So let me get this straight," Officer Crowell stated after hearing me explain everything. "You went over there willingly and at a late hour. You danced around in front of this video camera, but then you thought he turned it off.

You supposedly said no; however, you never came forward that night. Now that there's a recording, you're claiming that he raped you, even though after the incident you allowed this guy to take you home. Then even when you got home, you never came into the police station or called us. Is that what you're saying?"

I just dropped my head. Once again I had gotten in my own way. As big, bad, and tough as I thought I was, when I needed to be strong, I was weak.

The officer scolded, "You should have come and gotten a rape kit. After all this time, there is no evidence. Even the video you're talking about … did you bring it here so we can have it analyzed to see if he altered it in any way?"

"What are you saying, sir? That I wasn't raped?" I cried.

He looked at me with cold eyes and commanded, "Calm down, miss. I just want to make sure that you know what you're doing. Rape is a serious allegation."

"Raping someone is a serious crime," I responded boldly. "I was traumatized, sir. I can't explain why I didn't come forward other than to say I was scared. That might be a pathetic excuse, and I know it seems convenient that I want to talk now, but this guy is a monster and needs to be stopped. If you don't want to help me—"

Before I could finish, the door opened and there was a lady standing there. "I hear there is a young lady reporting a rape. John, I can take over from here."

"Oh no. He's made it pretty clear that I have no case," I cried. "I have only myself to blame."

"No, I didn't say that," Officer Crowell insisted. Like he was on my side. Right.

"John, you didn't tell her that, did you?"

I looked at him like, *Be real, man. You basically said that. I dare you to tell this woman that it is not what you said*. Seeing that he was not going to confess, I stood to my feet.

"I've had enough. I'm not going to be humiliated any more. I made my decision even though it was a bad one. I am the one who decided to keep it all to myself. I'll have to live with this," I said. I tried leaving the cold interrogation room.

"Wait, please, I would like to talk to you," the nicer lady said.

"Talk to him. He knows everything," I said before fleeing out the front doors of the police station.

My friends asked a million questions. I just put my hands over my ears. My head was killing me. This was too much, and I was too stressed out.

"Talk to us. Eva, you got to talk to us. You have to say something," Charli said.

"They didn't believe me, okay? I waited too long. It was my fault," I finally told them.

Charli would not let up. "Well, let's go by a hospital. You can't just give up."

"The way I feel right now, Charli, I have no fight in me. You guys be better than me, okay? No short dresses, no low-cut shirts, no wearing shirts without bras, and wear your panties at all times," I ordered.

"It wasn't your fault," Randal responded.

"Yeah, you didn't deserve this, sis," Ella said.

"Where is his tail? Let's go kill him," Charli commanded.

In a tired voice, I said, "You guys, it's late. We all need to be somewhere safe and not on the streets trying to get revenge on some guy who, according to the cops, doesn't deserve it. I know you can't understand it, but I'm tired. Please, just let me be. Just drop it. Leave me alone about it, please."

The ride back to my place was one that we made in silence. Rico took so much from me. I saw no way I could ever get it back.

"Why am I even here?" I thought to myself. I sat in the pew at Lakeside Baptist Church on Sunday morning.

My mom worked all night and got me and my sister up to go to church. She was taking all that I was going through personally. I guess she thought it was possible to pray my troubles away. I told them I needed to go to the ladies room, but I made my way into the smaller sanctuary within the mega-church.

I did not know if I believed in God or not. I never called on Him before, but I figured now was the time to try out some force bigger than myself. I needed a change of heart. I needed a change of mind. I needed a change to my soul because everything in me felt so dark and desolate.

I did not know how to pray. Honestly, I was not really feeling it. I was just thankful for the darkness. I placed my head on the pew in front of me to rest. Before I could express any kind of emotion, the door opened. I was freaking out because there were too many shadows. I could not see a clear image. I did not know who was there. I did the only thing I knew to do: hide. I saw a faint image sit in the pew in front of me. I eased up some when I heard weeping. It was not a female voice. It wasn't an older voice.

It was a young guy calling out, "Why? Why did this have to happen to me? I was so young, and I didn't do anything wrong. I tried to pretend it didn't happen, but I know it did. Why weren't You there? Why wasn't my father there? No one protected me, and now I got to deal with this alone."

After listening, I realized it was Landon's voice. What was he talking about? What did he have to live with? Why was he so upset?

Landon continued, "He touched me. He violated me. He molested me."

"Dang, what!?" I screamed. I was unable to hold back the way the words affected me.

“Who’s there?” Landon demanded in a surprised-upset tone rolled into one.

“I’m … I’m sorry,” I said quickly. I felt terrible that I’d inadvertently invaded his private space.

Unlike me, Landon was very familiar with the church; after all, his dad was the pastor. He ran to the back of the room and flicked on a light. He was stunned to find me there.

“You?” Landon growled in an irritated voice. “What are you doing in here, Eva?”

I walked toward him, wanting to wipe his eyes. Landon was always a jokester, the man who made the room light up, the optimist, and the one full of energy. Now his world seemed as dark as mine.

I kept walking toward him and said, “You know why I’m here. The whole school does. I don’t know if I’m getting anything out of it. I don’t even know how to talk to God but listening to you—”

“I can’t believe you were eavesdropping.” He turned away.

Turning him back toward me, I grabbed the little spunk I had left and said, “I mean, you just came in here, and you didn't ask if there was anybody else in here. Technically, this was my space before it was yours."

He huffed and realized he had the wrong one on the wrong day. "Okay, calm down. I'm not saying you shouldn't be in here. I just wish you would've told me before I start telling all of my life, like I wanted anybody to know."

"I understand. I don't exactly get what happened to you. That is your business. But I do apologize for being so caught up in everything and not letting you know I was in here, but something terrible happened to me too. I don't just mean the video that's been floating around. Something far worse, Landon. I was scared. I didn't know who was coming in. I'm just not the same anymore." I sighed, backed up, and lowered my head.

"You can't sleep?" he asked in a manner that connected to my pain.

"Nor eat," I replied.

"Or relax," he said.

"Yeah," I responded, knowing he was getting what I was going through so much that I knew we were in the same gloomy place.

He stepped closer to me, and he could see I was fragile too. "Do you want to talk?"

"I don't know," I said as tears pooled in my eyes.

"I understand," he said. A single tear fell from his eye.

I stepped closer. Seeing him crying bothered me. I wiped his face.

"Maybe we should," I said. His tears touched me to my core.

"Maybe we should what?" he asked, trying to be strong.

"Open up to each other," I stated. I truly wanted to connect. "You already know a little about what I'm going through, but you don't fully understand it. I don't even understand it, and I hope you can't relate to it. I was raped."

"Nah, Eva, don't even tell me that. Talk to me. Tell me what happened."

The way he said it connected to my heart. It was not a demand, but I could feel his need.

I had the same one: wishing that I was not in this alone, wishing that I had someone who understood, and needing someone to bounce it all off of who could rationalize it. I longed for someone to make sense of it for me, someone who truly understood. Maybe Landon was that person. Maybe I came to that small sanctuary to find a friend. Both of us sat in the back pew.

I started. "The guy who sent that video ... I went out on a date with him. He wanted to take things further than I did. I said no, but he didn't listen. He edited that video to make it look like I wanted it, but I didn't. I don't know why that happened to me, but it woke me up. I was not taking life seriously. Now I'm fully conscious of my choices."

"I understand," Landon affirmed. "We got a substitute teacher who was at our school."

"Yeah," I said, remembering Mr. Gunn, the cute guy who subbed in math class.

Landon started talking in a serious tone. "He was my little league football coach when I was ten. He took me to games. He bought me ice cream after practice when my dad was just building this facility. My father was so busy, but the coach made time for me always. My dad was so grateful he never even questioned. He never even asked what we did. In middle school, I never even played football because I was so traumatized by something that happened to me in the fifth grade."

"No, please don't let Landon say that Gunn raped him," I thought, but I knew what was coming. I couldn't interrupt Landon; he let me have *my* say.

He was talking. He was sharing, and I needed to care. Unfortunately, he confirmed my worst fears. He did understand what I was going through. We had both been violated. We had both been taken advantage of. What I didn't know was, where did each of us go from here? Could either of us ever heal? I knew we were both very broken.

CHAPTER 6

Resolve Errors

You didn't have to take me to breakfast, Landon," I said as the two of us sat in a nearby Waffle House.

We had both needed to get out of that church. Neither of us wanted to go back into the service, even though some positive words may have helped.

"It's the least I could do for … never mind," Landon responded.

Without thinking, I placed my hand on his. He gripped it real tight. We held a stare that connected somewhere deep down.

Letting go of his hand, I said, "I'm glad we can talk."

Landon said, "Yeah, it's good to open up. It's been a lot seeing that man hanging around my little brother's football team and having to confront my own memories that I tried to suppress. I don't want this to come out. I don't want to give any of my friends a reason to ask me if I'm gay. Unlike my boys, I haven't had a steady girlfriend yet."

"Well, since this has happened to me, I know what you mean about people hearing what they wanna hear and making assumptions," I said. "It's the same with me. People think because I dress a certain way or talk a certain way or—"

"Went out with a bunch of college guys," Landon cut in.

I couldn't get mad. The shoe fit and I had to wear it. My reputation was less than stellar. Now I wanted the way people viewed me to change for the better.

"Why wouldn't you ever give us guys in your grade a chance?" Landon asked.

I blurted out, "Because you all seem so immature."

"Wow, you're talking about me now," Landon teased, flexing his muscles.

I smiled, "I guess I missed the fact that some of you have grown up."

He smiled back. Landon had me blushing. This was crazy and awkward. To avoid the weird moment, we kept eating. Both of us were chowing down. All we had been going through lately, neither of us had probably eaten a lot. It was showing, as our food was gone in no time.

"What now?" I said to him. We sat there contemplating our lives, both wanting to get up out of the pit.

"I gotta talk to my dad. This all needs to come out. I want him to hear it from me. I don't know how he's gonna react. I wished worrying about his reaction didn't bother me, but it does."

"I know what you mean. My dad hates my guts right now. That's killing me," I confessed.

"Your dad just got married. I saw you here for his wedding. Weren't you standing up there with him? You had on your dress and stuff."

I wanted to comment, "You noticed that?" But then I remembered, when I bumped into him, he seemed pretty irritated. Now his demeanor made sense. Landon was not being a jerk or being rude, he actually was dealing with so much. And through all of that he remembered running into me.

As if reading my mind, he said, "I'm sorry. The couple of times I saw you in school and at the church, I wasn't even looking where I was going. Dumb me bumped straight into you. Forgive me. You now understand why I was so stressed out and preoccupied."

This guy was being nice to me. We were talking. He was caring. I didn't deserve that. I could not face him.

He turned my face toward his and said, "You know you didn't bring anything that happen to you on yourself, right? I mean, I hear you joking about your clothes and your attitude and how others perceive you. You got the right to say no. You're able to change your mind."

"Obviously, I wasn't."

"No, obviously he didn't *hear* you. Now you gotta take care of that. Your parents know?"

"My mom does."

"You call the police yet?"

"Ha-ha," I laughed.

It was not funny. However, I could not stop laughing. Police were supposed to be helpful.

The ones I dealt with were the ones who needed to not be in law enforcement.

"Talk to me," he said in a gentle way.

"I didn't go to the police right away, and when I did, I got a jerk of a cop who said I had no claim since I waited."

"What?!"

"My dad's an attorney. If I could just talk to him, maybe he could see if there's something legally I could do. I don't want Rico to be able to do this to anyone else. I couldn't stand it if he attacked someone else, and I never reported what happened to me."

"Rico. I remembered him from school a couple of years ago. What a jerk. I don't understand why people don't go away for college. I lived in the ATL all my life. While it's always gonna be in my blood, there's more to the world than here."

We were done with our delicious meal. Church was letting out, but Landon wasn't walking inside. He huffed. I realized I did not want him to struggle with confronting this anymore.

I held his hand and said, "Let's go talk to your dad. After we talk to him, you can help me talk to mine. Deal?"

He looked over at me and asked, "You'd do that?"

"We can keep each other calm. Together, rational heads prevail, right?"

"Both Rico and crazy Gunn need to be in orange jumpsuits," Landon joked. "Meet me at my dad's office in ten, okay?"

Watching him walk away, I was thankful for my new buddy. I needed to find my mom and sister so I could meet back up with Landon. As soon as I found them, my mom threw her arms around me.

My mom said, "Are you okay, sweetie?"

Nodding, I said, "Yes, ma'am. I'ma catch up with you guys later. I'm going to talk to Pastor King."

"How are you going to get home?" Ella asked. "And can you even see Pastor King?"

"Landon said he'd bring me, and I'm going to talk to his dad with him," I explained.

"Oh yes. Oh, that's good, talk to the pastor," my mom said. She hugged me before walking over to one of her friends.

"Landon knows?" my sister leaned over and whispered.

"Long story."

"Well, it seems like a good story. You're a lil' perked up. You've got pep in your step. You wanna talk to the pastor. I'm all for whatever Landon said to get you in this mood. He's a great guy—Leo's best friend. You have no issues from me." Ella grinned.

I could tell she was thinking something more than was there. I threw up my hand and turned to head out. Landon was turning out to be cooler than I thought.

My sister was also right about asking me if I could get to see Pastor King. When I got to his office, it was like a whole other complex. Getting in was like Fort Knox or something. Armor bearers and the three secretaries were all looking at me like, *Ahh, why are you up here?* This was church, and I was sure my pastor preached a great sermon. Why couldn't I just say thank you for blessing me? Did I need an appointment and status to be able to do that?

"She's with me, you guys," Landon said, rescuing me from the wolves.

They parted and let me pass. Landon grabbed my hand and pulled me. The next thing

I knew, we were sitting in a beautiful, lavish space.

"Okay, son, you know I'm preaching in Savannah. I must get on the road in a minute. What's this about?" Pastor King said from behind his large mahogany desk.

"Dad, you're not going to say hello to my friend Eva?"

Pastor noticed me for the first time. "Hello, Eva. Please forgive me for being so rude. My son said he had something to talk to me about. He steps in, then out, and then you come in. Is this about you two?"

I thought, "Sir, why can't people talk to you? Why can't people have easier access to you? Why do you make it so difficult? Why couldn't you preach at my dad's wedding? Why aren't you more involved in your son's life? He's breaking, and you can't even see it. What good does it do to be famous and inspire lots of people, when you have no follow-up and are not truly making an impact on anyone?" But I sat there, smiled, and gave the politically correct response.

"Hello, sir. No, this is just about Landon. I'm only here for support," I said. Landon's father immediately became concerned and sat to hear from his son.

All the harsh things I thought about Pastor King being too busy for the world changed in a blink of an eye. When Landon opened up and told his dad his story, his father became shaken with grief over what he heard. My heart went out to both of them.

"I'm gonna cancel my plans for today. We're gonna deal with this right now," Pastor King commanded.

"No, Dad, go preach," Landon replied, knowing his dad was important to many. "Besides, I need to go somewhere with Eva."

Pastor King came over to his son and placed his hand on his shoulder. "My boy, I should have known. I should have been there. I'm sorry."

About an hour later, Landon dropped me off. My story didn't end as well as his did. Landon thought it was best if I call my dad first before we went over there. My dad and Samantha were not even home. They had taken the baby to Samantha's relatives.

When we finally spoke on the phone, my dad didn't believe me when I said I was raped.

d me of concocting another ploy to try lose to him and cause problems in his iage. This devastated me.

Landon repeatedly tried telling me it was not my fault and it would be okay. He also said he wanted to help me through all this. Problem was, I thought it *was* my fault. My rep was so bad that even my dad did not believe me. How could Landon help me? Frustrated, I got out of the car and slammed the door. I didn't even look back at Landon, thank him, or nothing. As kind as he had been, that was not right. But that was real.

We had an away game at our rival's school not too far away. Mays High School had a rich tradition in the city of Atlanta. They had a good football team this year. However, our boys were ready to beat them. I was not ready to cheer.

My mother contacted Coach Woods and explained to her everything that had happened to me, just in case I had a meltdown. My four besties, including my sister, said they would take my secret to their graves. As I looked at each of them, I could tell it was only a matter of time before one of them popped. It was not a situation where they wanted to spread my business and hurt me. No, it was quite the opposite. They wanted to protect me. When we walked to the bathroom, we could hear crowds of people whispering about me.

"That's that girl in the video," one girl smirked.

"Yeah, she was doing all kinds of things I didn't even know people could do," another one joked.

"Look here, shawty, I wanna talk to you," one guy called out. But I briskly moved by. "Oh, don't walk away like you all that now. We done seen everything."

There was one nasty comment after another. I wrongfully assumed at an away game that I would not have to be in front of my peers, but because this was Mays, it seemed everyone from Lockwood was there. I felt everyone was ragging on me.

Thankfully, the game was going good. The Lions were kicking on all cylinders, and the defense was keeping Mays from scoring. Special teams were putting us in great field position, and Waxton was doing his thing, running the ball. That running also ran the clock down, which was really good for me. I felt like a punching bag, there for anybody who wanted to take a shot at me. My girls were getting tired of it.

Charli came over to me and said, "People need to know what happened to you. If they did, they would keep their mouths shut, but they don't and you're not gonna tell them."

We walked to the bus after we won 18–3. We made three touchdowns. The only flaw on our team was that our kicker couldn't get the extra points. We had a new guy who everyone said supposedly was great at kicking. He had NFL potential, but he wasn't eligible *and* he was white. Being white wasn't a bad thing, but he just seemed uncomfortable at our predominately black school. Randal even tripped sometimes about feeling uneasy being more than one race. I didn't see the big deal with her argument. Anytime you had a little bit of chocolate in you, the world considered you black.

I wanted to be home and put the covers over my head. So nobody could see me. So nobody knew what I was going through. So nobody could get in my case. I knew I had to open my mouth and help others, but I couldn't.

I saw a girl walking with a guy who was grabbing on her. Though she jerked away, he continued. Then there was a freshmen flirting with a senior. She might think it was innocent, but what if he took her up on the flirtation. She would not have a prayer. And what about the nerd in the crowd of hunks wishing he had more muscles and could have his way with the ladies? I wanted to scream out, "Don't rush it! You'll mature in time."

People had to stop thinking they were entitled to pressure people to give them what they wanted, and to be so dominant that they became violent. I was so choked up with these new realizations that I could not speak. I got on the bus and rode home in silence.

As soon as we got off the bus, the fall night air felt so good on my face. I just ran. I forgot I needed a way home. I forgot the lights in our stadium were off. I forgot that what I was doing there made no sense. I needed to think. Placing my head on the steel stadium bleachers, I took a rest for a second. I wanted my life to be better.

I heard my sister call out, "Eva, please. Where are you?"

Leo was with her and he shouted. “Eva! We’re looking for you. Just let us know you’re all right.”

Then I jumped as someone touched me. I felt a strong arm against my shoulder. I turned around, ready to sock the guy. It was Landon. I exhaled deeply.

“What’s going on with you? Why do you have us all worried?”

Landon sat down beside me, and I buried my head in his chest and said, “I just can’t take this. It hurts so bad. I was the strongest person I knew, Landon. Now I feel like an infant. Every little thing somebody says bothers me. I hate myself. I don’t know how to resolve any of this.”

“Well, acknowledging your feelings is the first step. Running away is not gonna solve crap,” Landon maintained. I tried to pull away, but he held me tight. “Look, I told you I’m gonna be there for you.”

“How can you help me when you’re sinking too?”

“Let’s get in that boat, patch the thing up, and help each other survive,” Landon suggested. “I’m down if you’re down.”

I was hesitant. "I don't know if I want everybody knowing about this. Leo's out here helping find me. He must know something is wrong. He's your boy and my sister's boyfriend. What does he know?"

"I don't know, but I haven't told him nothing. If he knows anything, it's 'cause your sister probably needed someone to talk to, and with you shutting everybody out, can you blame her? All guys aren't bad, Eva. Don't go through this alone."

"You're sweet to wanna help," I affirmed. But I backed away, knowing that the two of us couldn't be anything more than just friends. We were both too fragile for anything else. I didn't want to give him the wrong idea. His friendship was enough.

Sensing I was overwhelmed, the caring hunk in front of me said, "Let's just get out of this dark stadium. Take it one day at a time."

"I feel so unworthy to keep going on. You just don't understand," I said, explaining more than I had ever verbalized to anyone else.

"What? You wanna take your own life or something?" Landon asked. "It's not a new thought."

"You wanted to do that?" I asked.

"I gave a lot of thought to it. But where's the justice in that? What would that solve? That would give him even more power, which he doesn't deserve," Landon explained in a sweet tone. "But, Eva, we might be a little cowardly, but we are probably more courageous than we know. We just need to open up our mouths and roar to fight back the demons inside. We just need to keep building ourselves up when we wanna tear ourselves down. If we focus on the truth and not on the lies ... If we focus on the healing and not on the pain ... If we focus on what's in front of us and not what's behind … We can be stronger because of it and help others so they won't have to go through it. One of these days we'll say it was worth it."

"That's a day I can't see right now," I whispered.

"Here, let me lend you my glasses."

"You're not wearing any," I laughed.

"See, why you have to call me out on that? I thought I was."

We both smiled. I didn't even realize we were walking toward the parking lot because I was so in tune with what he was saying. Suddenly, Landon gently kissed my forehead. We were both a little shocked at the gesture. But then I smiled at him. When my sister saw me, she rushed up and hugged me like she had not seen me in weeks. Landon was talking to Leo. I looked over at my new friend and was grateful. He was right. I had the power to get over this. It was a mind thing, and I was going to win the battle within.

It is a wonderful thing to get a good night's rest. Landon helped me put things into perspective. I was only a victim if I wanted to stay a victim. If I wanted to triumph, that could be my fate as well. And that was the direction I was choosing.

Funny thing, though. As soon as you get ready to look at life in a positive direction, something smacks you dead in the face. It tells you it ain't gonna be that easy just moving on. I thought I could remember that night with Rico in vivid detail, but then there were patches that were vague. I recalled that Rico did not use protection, and that he made sure he had a real good time.

Was I safe from getting pregnant? Safe from getting a disease? I didn't know.

Immediately, I pulled my calendar from my purse and looked at the date of when my cycle should be coming on. There were two days to go, which meant I was with Rico in the middle of my cycle, and that was the danger zone. Heck, all of it was a danger zone.

I was beginning to freak out. I did feel like I normally do when it's time for my cycle. I was irritable, a little bloated, a bit tired, and my breasts were tender. The problem was, those were the same signs as the early stages of pregnancy. I was not nauseous, but would it be too early for that? Ugh, I was freaking myself out, which was crazy.

Quickly, I went to the bathroom because I just wanted to let out everything bad in me. I did not know what I was thinking because it was not like that was possible. If I was pregnant, using the restroom would not make that go away. But there I was on the toilet, trying nonetheless.

I started feeling really weird between my legs. It was a feeling I never felt before. On one side, I was raw. When I did a self-check, there was a raised bump, which hurt extremely bad. I didn't know what to do. I didn't know what it was, but my mom was home and so was my sister.

Ella seemed so fragile. Every time I talked to her about anything, she would go into panic mode. But I was panicking too. What if I had HIV? If that was the case, the best chance I had for living was early detection and getting some medication.

I came into my room after washing my hands, closed the door, and said to Ella, "Okay, I need you to stay calm."

"What?" she croaked.

"Something's not right. Something's feeling really weird. I need to talk to Mom, but I don't wanna freak her out either."

Ella's voice rose. "What are you talking about? What's going on?"

I shared my concerns and observations about my body. She went to the laptop in the kitchen and began to surf the Internet. She wanted answers.

After a while, she came back and said, "I don't know. It could be a whole bunch of stuff. You need to talk to Mom. She needs to check you out."

"Ugh, she hasn't checked me out since I was five. She's gonna make me go to some gynecologist, and I don't want nobody putting any cold, sterile metal in places it's not supposed to go. You know what I'm saying?"

"Listen, Eva, if something is going on with you, you need to find out what it is. It's Saturday morning, and Mom probably knows a clinic that's open."

"Huh?" I didn't want to go to the clinic. "No, forget it," I said.

"What's this about a clinic?" my mom passed our room and asked. I gave my sister a hard stare.

"Talk to me, girls. Who needs a doctor?"

Ella looked straight at me. "She needs to talk to you."

My mom then came in the room. "Eva, what's going on?"

Knowing my mother was not going to let up, I said, "I don't know, Mom. I just don't feel good down there. My period is due in a couple of days. But something feels weird."

"Mom, she said she's got a bump or sore or something *down there*. You need to check her out right now, Mom. Check her," Ella insisted.

She was starting to panic, and I was incapable of speaking for myself.

My mom wasted no time making a phone call, setting up an appointment, and getting me in to see a doctor. While I waited to see the doctor, I had some tests done. I hated having on the white paper gown and sitting on a cold table. The least you think the doctor would do was have the room warm.

Mom and Ella were with me the whole time. My mom made me laugh, saying, "Ah, Miss Ella, you have a boyfriend now. Do I have to get you checked out too?"

Ella's brown face turned red. She wasn't doing nothing, and I could tell. I just cracked up at her embarrassment.

"And why are you laughing?" my mom said to me. "Because I'm dead on?"

"No, because you're *so* far off," Ella cried. She did not want to be viewed as a bad girl.

"I'm not way far off. I seen how you have been looking at Leo," my mom said, sounding like a good girlfriend.

My sister had pretty much lost her mind for the guy, but I didn't have a problem with it because he was treating her right. Everybody knew he was crazy about her too. Funny thing was, Leo had never settled down until Ella. Although they were young, you could tell they were really into each other.

"Good," my mom said. "Keep the legs closed."

Hating where we were, I said, "Right, 'cause she's got enough to deal with with my legs open."

"Eva!" Mom scolded.

I didn't have to respond because the doctor came in. The way Dr. Frost was looking, I thought she was about to confirm I was either pregnant or dying. So I asked her if was I either. Then a smile brushed across her face.

The doctor became serious. "It's still a little early to tell if you are pregnant, even though we gave you the test. Thus far it is negative. And you're not dying. The bad news is you do have a venereal disease. It's called herpes, and it will not go away."

"What do you mean? I'm gonna have this sore forever?" I cried.

"Well, not in the form it is currently in. You'll have to take medication to keep it under control.

Some are taken orally, and there are also creams that will make the sore more bearable. Don't wear tight clothes because that will irritate it. When you don't take the medicine, an outbreak will come up. We don't know why the disease flares, and there are some reasons we don't understand."

"Will the sore always be in the same place?" I sobbed.

"It could, but it could also move around. You could have multiple sores. Thankfully, you caught this early. Do you know you are able to pass this on to others as well?"

"What?"

"Yes, if you feel a little irritable, it's the outbreak at its full stage, and you're contagious."

My mom stood up and hugged me tight.

"I recommend you get some counseling, and I'd like to see you in a couple weeks to test you again for some other things. I know this is hard and seems unfair with what you went through, but everyone goes on and lives healthy lives with this virus. I know you will too. It was a terrible thing that happened to you, but right now, the best thing we can do is get you treated, get you healthy, and resolve errors."

CHAPTER 7

Blissful Truth

"Okay, you guys, you don't have to fuss over me so," I commanded. My mother and sister were attending to my every need and driving me crazy.

My sister propped up my feet and said, "We just want to make sure you're comfortable."

My mom came and put a pillow behind me. "You've been through a lot," she sighed. "You deserve some pampering." Then she started massaging my back. She bent down and kissed me on the cheek. My sister took off my slippers and rubbed my feet through my socks.

"Okay, you guys," I giggled. "I'm okay, really."

It was Sunday evening. The school week was about to get started, but just having two days of whatever the medicine was called that the doctor gave me for my disease was helping. My mom and sister were making sure I was not stressed out. That was another thing the doctor said that would flare up an outbreak.

There was a knock on the door. My mother looked at my sister and said, "Now? It's nine. It is too late for Leo to be trying to come over here."

"That shouldn't be him, Mom. It's not Dr. Sapp, is it?" Ella teased.

"Wait, what? Am I missing something?" I questioned, knowing the last couple of weeks I'd been out of it.

My mom could have had lunch with Mrs. Obama, and I wouldn't have noticed the Secret Service come to pick her up. I was just that dazed. I had gone through a ton. The only person's business I could handle was my own.

"What are you talking about, Ella?" our mom, sounding very innocent, asked.

"Our principal's got the hots for our mom," Ella leaned over and told me.

"*I knew it*," I said, remembering him eyeing her like she was a biscuit dipped in hot gravy or something.

"I just invited him to Thanksgiving," Mom dismissed "Nothing more."

"Yeah, and ever since then you've been going around here cleaning, putting up drapes, and making this place a home," Ella replied. It was looking like HGTV in our apartment.

My mom replied, "We needed to fix it up. No big deal."

Ella chuckled. "Okay, if that's how you want to play it, fine with me."

Then the knock came again. The talk about Dr. Sapp made us forget that someone was even at the door. The three of us wondered who it was.

"Maybe that's our principal," I called out, playing with my mom.

"Yeah, maybe it is," Ella teased. My mom gave us a look that said, *Enough!*

Things were going really well for me until I saw my mother open the door. My dad was standing there with Samantha. What did *they* want? Were they coming over here to gloat? I had not seen him since he went off on me at the football game. Did he want to tell me off in front of her because she did not believe that he had taken care of the problem—me? If I had on jeans, I would have gone to my room, but I had on big boxers, so I just sat there, pulled the covers closer, and held a defiant glare.

"May we come in?" my dad asked my mom.

My mom could tell I was not feeling them. She said, "Eva's resting. We certainly would've loved to know you were coming. She's not really fully dressed."

Surprisingly, Samantha stepped forward and said, "It's my fault. This is impromptu. I really wanted to come by."

"I wanted to come by too," my dad concurred. "We were nearby, and we really want to speak to Eva, if that's okay."

"Where's my little brother?" Ella said to the newlyweds.

"Do you mean Evan or El?"

"Oh my gosh! The baby's name is similar to mine," Ella cried. She rushed to them for hugs.

Good for her, she was friends with the two of them. I really could not relate to either one of them, regardless of the fact that one was my father. My dad said something to my mom because Mom and Ella disappeared into the kitchen.

Not wanting to be alone with my dad and his bride, I quickly uttered, "You didn't have to come all the way over here, Dad. You could've put Samantha on the phone, and I would've told her that you went off on me and told me to never bother y'all again. Now if that's it, I'd like to rest."

Teardrops were visible in Samantha's eyes. "I came to ask you to forgive me."

Truly surprised and confused, I murmured, "Huh?"

Samantha continued, "I should've known you were so similar to me. Spunky, sassy, attractive, indiscreet, flashy, showing poor judgment, and then letting all of that backfire in your face."

Where was Samantha going with this? I did not understand what she was trying to say to me. She was getting really emotional with me, and whatever it was about, it seemed pretty serious.

"When your dad told me what happened to you ... it brought up a lot of bad memories for me. When I was in college, I was extremely popular. I was a majorette in the band at Howard. I never pledged a sorority; those girls hated on me a little too much."

"Just tell her," my d...
Samantha was going all ...
world just to get to some poin...

"There was this guy who al...
and was interning with the legisla...
me he could help move my career f... He told me that he could get me a job in the White House. He was going to help me with my résumé. I admit, I liked him at first, but he took things too far, too fast. I tried to break things off. Things got ugly, and I was never the same." She sat down on the sofa next to me and held my hand. "What happened to you was not your fault. I didn't even have to know all the details, but I believe you one hundred percent. I'm sorry I didn't tell you my story, because I saw where you were headed. Women have to do a better job of encouraging one another. You trusted the wrong guy, and it cost you. Back then, I didn't know legal folks. Now, I am in the legal profession. I want to help you. I work for the district attorney. We can prosecute the horrible guy who did this."

My dad said, "I should've believed you too, pumpkin. I was just so clouded by my own mistakes that I didn't see what you were saying.

your father, but I wasn't there for you. I know that you've been doing outlandish things because you were starved for attention from your father. I just wasn't there for you," he repeated. "I'll never be able to make that up to you."

"Daddy, you don't have to say that," I exclaimed. Their empathy was affirming and overwhelming.

At that moment, I was really grateful that I had two lawyers who believed me. My dad had not been there during my upbringing. However, he was standing before me in my time of need. I reached up and hugged him.

"We're going to get him," my dad declared. Then he tightened the embrace we shared.

I pulled back as I remembered I'd already tried this and was unsuccessful. "I don't know how. I went to the cops, and they told me I had no evidence."

"Yeah, you told me that, but you said there was some tape going around. We just need to get a copy of that," my father said.

Samantha looked at me and said, "Look, I know it's been rough with people accusing you of bringing this on yourself and others not believing your story. Dealing with this internally has to be so difficult. It took me years to get better because I had no one to talk to. I know things have been rough between us, and you must feel like you've lost your father all over again. Let's scratch all that history and drama. Let's start from the beginning … from a place of love. Because if you're okay with it, I want to make sure you have everything you need to overcome this."

Ready to start anew with my stepmother, I reached up and hugged her. I could see my dad over her shoulder, and I mouthed, "Thank you." Rico took a lot from me, and now it seemed like I was starting to get some great things back.

We were having two assemblies at school as part of the Stand Against Violence Campaign. The school district brought in a team of professionals from around the country to talk to us about bullying, gang violence, self-mutilation, and rape. The boys were going to be in the gym, and the girls were in the auditorium. Almost everybody was excited because nobody had to be in class. I was not as thrilled to go hear a bunch of people talk about these tough subjects.

But we did have an out. If you did not want to attend the assembly, you could go to the library and study. Since Ella showed me how to buckle down and really study, I realized I was doing myself an injustice by not working hard in school. I was caught up with my work, but I could've read ahead or gone over some things that I missed; however, as much as I did not want to be in the auditorium and talk about violence, I had an overwhelming feeling that I really did need to be there.

Someone touched my waist and I jerked. I looked around and saw it was Landon. My fist was about to hit him.

"I'm sorry. I'm sorry," he apologized.

"Boy, you scared me!"

"I was just playing."

"Playing? You know I'm on edge."

"Right, sorry, I wasn't thinking," he said. "You doing okay?"

"Mr. King and Miss Blount, y'all need to get where y'all are supposed to be and pronto," Dr. Sapp barked.

"See you later," Landon whispered.

Before I went into the auditorium, Dr. Sapp said, "Tell your mom I'm looking forward to Thanksgiving dinner."

"Oh, I'll tell her," I said slyly. I wanted to tell him that she was looking forward to it too. Something was definitely going on there.

There was a panel made up of three professionals in the assembly: one lady was a psychologist, another lady was a policewoman, and the third was a medical doctor. We were not guys, but everyone was so loud and hyped up. Girls were being rude to the presenters and not even paying attention to the good information that was being shared.

Dr. Sapp was not in there with us because he was with the boys. Our assistant principal was in the back, but no one respected him because he was such a wimp. He tried to get people to calm down, but folks got louder.

Finally, I just stood and hollered, "Hey, everyone calm down. They're trying to help you. They're trying to tell you stuff that you need to hear. You guys need to calm down and listen."

"What do you care?" somebody yelled out.

"Yeah, tramp, what do you know about it with the way you give it up?" another person hollered.

"I know a lot about it, okay?"

"Young lady?" one of the speakers interrupted. "Would you like to come up front and tell your story?"

Ella was sitting next to me. She tugged on my jacket and said, "You don't have to."

I turned to her and declared, "I want to."

As I walked to the stage, the medical doctor gave statistics. "Did you know one in seven students in grades K–12 are either a bully or a victim of bullying. It is estimated that one hundred sixty thousand children miss school daily because of the fear of violence or intimidation by other students. A review of surveys found that between thirty and forty percent of male teens and sixteen to thirty-two percent of female teens say they have committed a serious violent offense by the age of seventeen. Another staggering statistic is that suicide is the third leading cause of death among teenagers. Over fifteen hundred teens kill themselves each year."

The policewoman, who looked familiar, added, "Yes, more than three in five youth suicides involve firearms. Every two minutes someone in America is being sexually assaulted, and every year there are about two hundred thirteen thousand victims of sexual assault. Forty-four percent of rape victims are under age eighteen and eighty percent are under age thirty. Fifty-seven percent of the rapes happened while on dates. Sixty percent of sexual assaults are not reported to police, and fifteen out of sixteen rapists will never spend a day in jail. Approximately two-thirds of assaults are committed by someone known to the victim, and thirty-eight percent of rapists are friends or acquaintances."

Charli yelled out, "Yeah, when you go to the cops and they give you a hard time, why tell? Why bother?"

The policewoman said, "Officers are not perfect. Sometimes you catch them in a tough moment. If you ever feel like one is not hearing you out, don't leave. Find another one. We do care."

I got to the stage and became timid when I looked around the room. I breathed deep and knew I had to speak up. If ever there was a time for sassy Eva to show up, it was now. If I could help someone else be wiser, I needed to.

Finding the courage, I said, "I know y'all have probably heard about or saw the sexting scandal that involved me. What you don't know is that the video was manipulated. What you actually saw was an assault. A date rape. I'm getting counseling to help me understand that it was not my fault. I said no. I just want to say to you guys that I thought I didn't need anybody to tell me anything. I thought my body was my greatest attribute, and that I needed to flaunt it to get what I wanted in this life."

I took a deep breath and continued, "I put myself in a tough situation. I went out with a guy who looked at me like all he wanted to do was have his way. I went out with him anyway, knowing that was not what I wanted. I went out with him late at night. I had skimpy clothes on. He raped me after I said no. I hurt myself. We're all getting older, and our hormones are changing. Slow your roll. Know who you're going out with. Be careful. If you end up in a situation you don't want to be in, go to the police immediately."

You could hear a pin drop in the room. Every girl had tuned in. Every girl understood how serious this was to me. Every female there knew date rape, teen violence, and self-mutilation was real and affecting girls at Lockwood High School. They needed to wake up and be more responsible. They needed to be better than I was.

The psychologist stood and said, "Thank you so much for sharing that."

As I went to my seat, I knew the girls were going to look at me differently. I knew I had put myself out there. I made myself so transparent, but that was my duty. If I could help one girl not go through what I went through, then telling the truth was worth it.

As soon as the assembly was over, I could not get out of the place. First the police officer came over and told me she remembered me and my friends coming to the station. She apologized and told me the officers had been lectured for being too cavalier.

Many girls were coming up to me and telling me their stories about how they went out with guys who they had reservations about, and now they knew not to go out with them again. Other girls, who had similar experiences to my own, were thankful that they were not alone. Many girls thanked me for my transparency.

I was happy to be making lemonade out of lemons. We females had to stick together. For so long I tried so hard to set myself apart from them, but now I knew I was one of them through and through—vulnerable, emotional, and fragile. Yet my strength was resilient, and if all girls found and lived in a healthy place, we could keep one another lifted up.

When we headed out of the assembly, Ella ran up and gave me a huge hug. "I'm so proud of you, sis. That was excellent."

"Thanks, girl," I said as I realized I needed to share with her how much she meant to me. "And thanks for being there for me. I know I haven't always been the easiest sister to have, but you're the only one I'd ever want."

Staring back at my mirror image, I hugged her so hard. She was actually the better part of me. Because I embraced that, I was becoming better.

"He asked me," Ella giggled. I could tell that she could not hold in her excitement.

"He asked you what?"

"To the homecoming dance."

"Why is homecoming at the end of our season? That is crazy," I commented.

"I know, right? My Leo asked me." Ella twirled. "At first he said he didn't want to go, but then he asked me."

"Girl, you knew he was gonna ask you, so don't even trip."

"You've got to go too," Ella responded.

Faster than a track runner takes off when the starter gun fires, I scoffed, "Uh, no."

"No, I'm serious, sis. You don't have to worry about a date or anything. You can go stag."

"Yeah, I'm thinking about going by myself," Randal interrupted. She put her arm in mine.

"It's not that; it's just that I don't wanna—"

Before I even got a chance to continue to explain my reasons why I did not want to attend, Dr. Sapp came up to me and ordered, "Eva Blount, I need to see you in my office please."

My sister, feeling giddy, pointed directly at me, making sure he did not get us confused. She did not want to go back to ISS, but I did not want to go to his office again. What had I done? It dawned on me as I walked to his office that this was about the video floating around on people's cell phones. I was ready for Dr. Sapp. Truth was, I had nothing to do with it. I had done all I could to stop it, and I did not have to defend myself.

Before I could state my case, I saw my mom. "I was so excited to see you. I just had to get you out of class. You won't believe this."

"What, Mom, what?" Then I thought to myself, "You two are getting married?"

She explained, "They arrested Rico this morning. Your dad called me. We're gonna get this thing behind you, baby. I just want to let you know the cops believe you and so does the prosecutor. Samantha came through."

"Still, Mom, I'm the only one. It'll be my word against his."

She said, "No, baby. He created that tape, and then he sent it. You are still a minor. That is against the law. He's going to get some time. Are you going to be all right if you have to testify?"

If I never had to see Rico again, I would be so relieved. However, because I knew I had to put him away, I was ready to face him. He needed to know consequences came with his evil actions.

"Yes, ma'am," I affirmed. "I am definitely ready to testify."

"That's what I'm talking about," she encouraged. "My girl! That strength and fight in you I love so much is still there."

"You love it?" I questioned, feeling like she'd always detested my ways. "I thought you hated that I was so brash and sassy."

"In everything we need moderation. Too many sweets can make you sick, but do I want you to be meek and soft spoken? No. One of us in the household with that role is enough."

We both laughed, thinking of dear Ella. "I'm proud of you, baby. Understand that you don't have to be so hard, so tough, and have the wall up so high that you end up hurting yourself."

"I know, Mom. I've learned so much. I just spoke at the assembly and talked to other girls about what I have been through."

"Wow, you did? That was so brave, honey."

"Yeah, at first I didn't want to, but I figured if I could help anyone else be smarter and wiser, then maybe that's why I went through all of this. My reputation was shot anyhow; everyone's gonna look at me cross-eyed."

"So what? You're a wonderful person to put everyone else's needs over your own. I was behind you whether you decided to keep this to yourself or shout it from the rooftops, but I think this is a great decision. You blessed others, and that's always a good thing."

"So why do I care about how they perceive me or how they look at me or what they think about me? Ugh, Mom, none of this was ever me. Now I'm not so tough."

"Baby, you're tougher than you think. To actually stand up for what you believe in is laudable. If I had a medal, I'd give it to you, but for now I'll just give you another hug. Can I do that?"

"Yes, ma'am," I laughed.

I saw Dr. Sapp looking in on us. Though he had given us privacy, he was checking my mom out. I headed to the door to get to class.

"So what are you going to do about that one?" I said, indicating Dr. Sapp, who turned away quickly, trying to look like he was not looking at all.

"What do *you* think about that?" she asked.

"I know the way you've been cleaning and prepping our apartment. You like him."

She said, "Yeah, you know me, which is weird because we haven't really gotten a chance to talk."

"Go talk to him," I stated.

Surprised and smiling, she questioned, "You'd approve?"

"One thing I've learned is that you've got to take dating slow. Besides, you deserve happiness, Mom. Dr. Sapp is one of the good guys. I'll let y'all talk. I'll see you later. And thanks for telling me about the case. Things do work out."

My mom blew a kiss my way. When I exited, I smiled wildly at Dr. Sapp. I gave him a thumbs-up. He squinted. I nodded, letting him know that I knew and approved of him dating my mom.

When we got to our last class of the day, it was time to elect people for homecoming court. Of course, I put down my sister. Landon and I had English class together. Because we'd been in our own worlds for the past two weeks, I had forgotten that we were classmates until he came up to me and touched my shoulder.

"Hey."

"Hey," I said.

"Everybody's been talking about how you inspired them."

"I wasn't going to say anything, but I just felt I had to. But I think you've got something to feel good about too. I saw that math sub being removed from school first thing this morning. Was that your doing?"

"Could be." Landon looked at me with serious eyes. "Well, I know it meant something to folks for you to stand up and tell your story."

"I hope so," I told him.

"So, um, this dance next week ... are you going?"

"No, I'm still chilling. Low profile, you know. Why?" I asked, thinking he probably was not going to go either.

He said, "You know, I've just been hoping that you've been okay. It's been occupying my mind so much that I haven't even had time enough to focus on my own problems. You've been a great diversion."

"Well, I'm glad, I guess," I said.

"So I thought you could put a smile on my face if you would accompany me to the dance, but if you're not going, I can totally understand why."

"No, if you're gonna go, then I'd love to."

Our teacher allowed us to talk if we kept it low since the results of the elections would be announced before the period was over. Landon and I laughed and joked about nothing. I could not speak for him, but for me, it was the first time in a long time I felt normal. No eyes were watching me. No one was judging me. I was just a girl laughing with a guy as teens should do.

Dr. Sapp got on the intercom and announced the homecoming court. One freshman, one sophomore, and one junior would represent the court, and there were five seniors who would be up for homecoming queen with the winner being announced the night of homecoming.

I was not even paying attention but then he said, "Eva Blount, congratulations for being the junior class representative on the court."

I was blown away. Folks in my junior class picked me. I felt so unworthy. Maybe because I showed them that I was imperfect, they chose me to be their princess. Coming clean and sharing the darkest parts of me perhaps had helped others to not go down my path. My confession was rewarding for me in many ways. I would be forever changed for the better by my dark experience. While I still had a lot of healing, I knew in my heart that I *was* worthy. I was not shattered by my experience, and I took joy in that blissful truth.

STEPHANIE PERRY MOORE is the author of many YA inspirational fiction titles, including the *Payton Skky* series, the *Laurel Shadrach* series, the *Perry Skky Jr.* series, the *Yasmin Peace* series, the *Faith Thomas Novelzine* series, the *Carmen Browne* series, the *Morgan Love* series, and the *Beta Gamma Pi* series. Mrs. Moore speaks with young people across the country, encouraging them to achieve every attainable dream. She currently lives in the greater Atlanta area with her husband, Derrick, and their three children. Visit her website at www.stephanieperrymoore.com.

WANT A DIFFERENT

point of view?

JUST *flip* THE BOOK!

BE REAL

Stephanie Perry Moore

& Derrick Moore

SADDLEBACK EDUCATIONAL PUBLISHING

BALLER SWAG

All That

No Hating

Do You

Be Real

Got Pride

ISBN-13: 978-1-61651-887-5
ISBN-10: 1-61651-887-1
eBook: 978-1-61247-621-6

Printed in Guangzhou, China
0712/CA21201000

16 15 14 13 12   1 2 3 4 5

To Mr. Greg Thornton and Mr. Matthew Parker

We never would have had a chance to start a writing career if you had not given us an opportunity. Thank you for being real enough to understand there was a market that needed our work. You both have been pioneers in the publishing industry and have made a difference in this world through your leadership. We are so grateful you cared enough to take a chance on us.

You are glorious gentlemen ...
we really hope we're making you proud!

ACKNOWLEDGEMENTS

When bad things happen to you, it is natural to surpass the disturbing pain. You don't want to dwell on the past. You want to pretend you imagined the tough situation. You may be afraid of folks' reactions if you open up. However, you cannot truly move toward greatness if you don't stand up to unfairness. Know your stance can change the world for the better and right wrongs.

Yes, it is easier said than done to confront your issues. However, know that trials come to make you stronger. Learn from the injustice done to you. Don't judge people. Don't put people down. Don't hurt people. The meaning we hope you to get from this title: be real about your circumstances. If you need help, seek it. If you need to lift someone else up, pull them up. If you have to expose lies to get to the truth, do it. You are stronger because you have gone through some stuff. Be confident. Be bold. Be real.

Here is vast thanks to those who help us be real.

Acknowledgements

To our parents: Dr. Franklin and Shirley Perry Sr. and Ann Redding, because you really raised us well, we can do the same for our kids.

To our publisher, especially Ashley Thompson, because you made sure the covers were real and captured the eye, we have a chance to reach many.

To our extended family: brothers, Dennis Perry and Victor Moore, sister, Sherry Moore, godparents, Walter and Marjorie Kimbrough, Jim and Deen Sanders, young nephews, Franklin Perry III, Kadarius Moore, and godsons, Danton Lynn, Dakari Jones, and Dorian Lee, because you are a part of us, we are able to be real and tell stories that hopefully will help readers take a stand.

To our assistants: Joy Spencer and Keisha King, because you all work so hard, we can be on time with the project.

To our friends who mean so much: Paul and Susan Johnson, Chan and Laurie Gailey, Antonio and Gloria London, Chett and Lakeba Williams, Jay and Deborah Spencer, Bobby and Sarah Lundy, Harry and Torian Colon, Byron and Kim Forest, Donald and Deborah Bradley, because you are in our lives, we can be real and help others.

To our teens: Dustyn, Sydni, and Sheldyn, because you are ours, we are doing our part to make sure your generation is happy and healthy.

To the media specialists, school administrators, teachers, and educational companies across the country who support us, especially the great folks in Georgia public schools, because you support our work, we are able to keep it real and impact many young people.

To our new readers, who we have faith will reach their goals, because you want to be better, you will work to be better.

And to our King, who blesses us daily, because You allowed us to go through so much, we are able to be real in our writing, which will hopefully move many.

CHAPTER 1

Remain True

Why do I have to take Logan to football practice?" I asked my father in an angry tone. "He's *your* son. Dang!"

"Boy, because I doggone said so. That's why you got a car, to help me and your mom out," my dad, the infamous Pastor Lawrence King, boldly said to me. "So slow your roll and quit being selfish. Logan looks up to you. Spend time with him."

Whatever he said was law. I understood he was the parent, but he never acted like it. As the Southeast's biggest mega-pastor with a growing congregation, he always claimed he had something to do for the Lord. It was not that I doubted him. I was certain that he was speaking at different

churches, meeting with publishers for his many inspirational books, working with a movie studio on an upcoming film, being with our choirs in the music studio to get ready for their upcoming album, and many other things. Oh yeah, he was busy. He was doing a ton of things, but he was *not* being a father.

It was almost the end of the football season, and my dad had not come to any of the Lockwood Lions' games. But his congregation would think he deserved an award for being the best parent of the year because he would talk about me in his sermons. What was hard about all of this was that I had to watch him do the same thing to my little brother, Logan. Logan was a fifth grader, excited to play little league football. My mom took him everywhere, but sometimes he wanted the males to go out there and support him. When that was the case, my dad passed the buck to me. Heck, I was more of a dad to Logan than my dad was, and that was just ridiculous.

I really was sick and tired of the big-time pastor hiding behind the cloth. "I got this to do for the Lord. I got that to do for God," he'd say over and over. I was so over his holier-than-thou

attitude. However, I knew I could not try my dad. I was set up pretty sweet. I was riding in a new, black Cadillac Escalade with fat rims and a tight sound system. I had a debit card with unlimited funds. On top of that, there was not a day that passed where my dad did not leave cash on my dresser. I always sported the latest cologne, kicks, and clothes, but what I really wanted was my parents.

Though my mom did way more for us than my dad, she could do lots more. She enjoyed being the first lady, and I could not blame her for sticking close to him, because over the years I'd grown up seeing many ladies do whatever they could to get their pastor to give them a little extra special prayer, if you know what I mean. With many people's marriages not making it, I did not want that to be the fate for my folks. So when they took trips here and there, part of me was happy she was with him. In those times, we had trusted church members who watched over us.

My dad's mom came around a lot too. She was the only one who could really get him straight. Last year she told me I needed to just tell him how much I wanted him to be more in my life. I

did what she said, but it didn't do any good; what I said went in one ear and out the other.

I pleaded with him to spend time with his boys. Showing me we weren't important, the next thing I knew he was dialing a number on his cell. Giving me a thin smile, my mom kissed me on the forehead. She looked me in the eye, and said, "Please, just take care of your brother for us. Get him to practice, stay there, get him something to eat after, and y'all come on back home. We'll be back later on."

"Yeah, whatever, Mom. Whatever y'all need me to do. Forget if I am tired from practice or have homework to do," I grumbled.

"Boy, please," my dad snapped. "All you gotta do is look at the book and you know the material. You're so smart, and the way that y'all are winning, I know Coach Strong isn't working you boys too hard. I'm coming to your game Friday."

I chuckled at his comment. I knew it would be snowing in Georgia in July before he took time to come to Lockwood's game. However, he seemed to feel good saying it, so I waved at them both as they headed out the door and waited for Logan to come so we could leave.

When I got into the car with my brother, I realized he was really growing up. He had always been the little baby of the family. All the church members would pass him around, talking about how cute he was. There he sat, looking back at me like a little man.

Logan said, "You didn't want to hang out with me, huh?"

"Huh?" I questioned.

He wanted to have big-boy talk. I did not know if I was ready for that. Logan wasn't looking away, though. He wanted the truth. Obviously, he'd overheard.

"Nah, it's not that I didn't want to hang with you; it's just that uh—"

"Don't try to clean it up. You ain't gotta lie to me. I know you got a life. Shoot, in my eyes you're more important than Dad. You the man in high school. That's all my friends talk about; the Lions football team and y'all winning the state championship. I just really wanted you to come to practice so you can see I got skills too."

"Okay," I thought, "who are you, and what have you done with my corny brother?" The dude had turned cool overnight. At that moment, I felt

really bad for wanting to push him off. Of all the folks in his life, he wanted to hang with me. He was excited about me. He wanted to show me he could ball.

"I owe you an apology, Logan," I confessed.

"You're saying sorry to me? Why?"

"For being too busy. You are my brother. I don't want you to think that you're a burden."

"Yeah, but I heard what you said to Mama and 'nem."

"Mama and 'nem? When you talking like this? When'd you become so cool?" I wondered out loud. Then I lightly shoved him in the arm.

"I've been watching you. I see you, Leo, and Blake hanging. I wanted to be like y'all for a long time. I'm tryna get my man card and hold it down like y'all."

"Boy, you ain't even out of elementary school," I said, popping him in the back of his head. "You better get your safety patrol belt."

"Ha-ha-ha, Landon got jokes," Logan stated sarcastically.

"Wow, Logan, you're growing up for real."

"Yep, so I know you got better stuff to do than hang with me at football practice. It's cool if you

just want to drop me off and come back and get me. We'll be out here for an hour and a half."

Knowing that I wanted to invest in Mini-Me, I said, "No, I'm staying. I'll be sitting in the bleachers, watching. You talking junk and saying you got skills, so I wanna see."

"That's what's up," my brother declared, putting his fist out for me to hit it, and when I did, he hit mine.

Logan grabbed his helmet and jogged onto the field with his peers. Though he might have acted like he was a big boy, seeing all the youngsters out there was very comical. He was still very young and so impressionable.

He was doing his thing. My brother was leading the way. The team was following his lead with warm ups. He really was following in my footsteps. He took the position on the far right as a wide receiver. I did not even know that. I thought he was playing quarterback. Then when he took off, he was super fast. Poor little corner could not even cover him.

I was proud, but still a little salty knowing if my dad could see this, he would be excited too. At that moment, I knew I was going to have to

make sure that my brother was there to watch me play. I did not realize that he was watching me and my boys. If I was his role model, I was going to take the job seriously.

With that in mind, I looked around the park and saw that there were a few jokers older than me watching the youngsters like they were trying to get in their ear. They seemed like they wanted to get them to sell dope and stuff. That was not going to be the case with Logan; he was already confident, and he was a King. But I still had to make sure nobody led him astray.

When Coach Brown called them all in to say they did a good job in practice, I walked over and started talking to the other parents who knew I played ball at Lockwood High. I guess my letterman's jacket was a dead giveaway.

I really appreciated that they were excited our team was doing so well. One lady, who was the mother of the quarterback, said, "I know Logan has got to be excited that he's got his big brother out here. He's never had his family members come to practice; this is great."

That got me down. That was going to change. It was not going to be like that anymore. However,

when I looked up and saw Logan's coach introducing a man who looked familiar, my heart stopped.

Coach Brown said, "This is Mr. Gunn. He used to coach football here some years ago, and he has now moved back to the area. He's going to be assisting me here this year. His team won a lot of tournaments, and I'm blessed to have him on the staff."

Coach Gunn waved, looked at my brother, extended his hand, and pulled my brother to him. At that moment, something inside of me snapped. I could not pretend or suppress past memories any more. That was the man who molested me, and he was not going to do the same to my little brother.

As hard as I tried to suppress the truth of what happened to me in fifth grade, now that I had come face to face with Mr. Gunn again, I was unable to do so. I lay in my bed with night sweats. Tossing and turning, I tried to tell myself what happened to me was not real. It was real, though. A man who was in a position to oversee me, to be a mentor to me, to help me, to be there for me ... took advantage of me.

I wanted to go and wake my brother up and ask him questions. Has anybody ever touched him inappropriately? Had he ever had scary sessions in the field house? Did he ever take showers with grown-ups? Did horseplay ever lead to acts of abuse?

I did not do that for two reasons: one, because it was two in the morning; and two, because I felt like I would have known if something crazy had happened to Logan. When life changed for me back then, I became withdrawn. I was angry. I was drastically different. He was such a happy kid. I could not let him go back to practice with that Coach Gunn being around. I could not let what happened to me happen to my brother, or any other kid for that matter.

Here in the silent house, alone in my room, I remembered everything clearly. After winning our last game of the season, Coach Gunn was supposed to take me home. It rained that day, and we were filthy. When everyone else was gone, he told me I was the hero, and I deserved a surprise. However, he said before he could take me anywhere special, we needed to clean up. He turned on the water and told me to hop in the shower

and be quick about it. It was so steamy that at first I did not know he jumped in the shower too. He felt my muscles and said I was growing nicely. Before I knew it, other things happened, but I would not let myself think about the details.

I became enraged all over again because it took me years to get past the disgusting incident. When it was time for the team banquet, I told my parents I was sick. Then I quit playing. That worked out for my dad because he never made the time to take me anywhere. I never had to face evil Coach Gunn again. In middle school, I did not play football because I did not trust those in charge. Last I heard, he moved to Alabama, but since he was back, and around children ... I was in a pickle.

"Leo, my man," this girlie dude named Carlen came up to my boy and crooned.

"What up, guy?" Leo asked, being real cool about not wanting to make too big of a deal about Carlen's sexual orientation.

Waxton, our starting running back, teased, "Dang, man, I didn't know you were swaying."

"Watch it," Leo threatened.

Waxton did chill. Leo was the same height as me. Both of us were pushing six four, but Leo was thick. I needed to stay lean so I could be light on my feet and move. Though Waxton was as talented as us and older than us, he was a shrimp. He was cool, but he could not be too cool to Leo or else he would get a busted lip.

Carlen was sashaying in front of us. "I didn't know you and him were cool," I commented.

"We were in in-school suspension together not too long ago. His thing ain't my thing, but he's a cool cat," Leo explained.

"Cool, man," I mumbled.

Carlen used to be tough when he was on the same little league football team with me and Leo. But when he came out in middle school, acting more feminine than most girls, I stayed far away. Deep down on the inside, I did not want what happened to me to change who I knew I was to become. I was a boy then. I wanted to be a man. While Carlen was now cool in his own skin, I did not want any part in that.

"My sister makes me so mad," Ella said as she came up to Leo. She was one of the cheerleaders and had a twin sister, Eva.

I could not believe my boy had a girl now. Leo was one of the biggest players in the school, other than me and Wax. Suddenly, he settled down with a cheerleader. Ella was fine; I had to give him that. She was a sweetie pie who melted the tough exterior of my boy.

"Calm down, calm down," he encouraged. He was all into what was going on with her. "Talk to me."

"It's my sister. People are saying that she was out in front of the school having sex and stuff, dang it," Ella voiced. My eyes widened as I could imagine her twin sister, sassy Eva, doing just what she was being accused of.

"Handle that. I'll talk to y'all later," I said to the two of them.

Ella did not even realize that I was walking with Leo. "Oh, I'm sorry, Landon. I'm just venting."

"Nah, that's your boy. Y'all talk. I'll catch up with you later, man."

"Yeah," Leo said as he gave me dap.

School was a cool place for me. I was slapping hands with the guys, flirting with some of the girls, and life was good. That was until I went

into my math class and the substitute turned around. It was Mr. Gunn. He did not notice that I was sitting there. He did not see me yesterday because I snatched Logan by his jersey, quickly got to the car, and sped off.

Thankfully, more people started to come in, and a girl sat in front of me. I slouched down in my chair. I did not want him to see my face. I did not want to see his eyes. Neither of us needed to remember, but when I heard his voice, how could I forget?

In a groggy tone, he directed, "All right, settle down, class. I'm Mr. Gunn. I'll be your substitute while your teacher is out on a maternity leave. So you better get used to me. I like to have fun, but I'm stern. Don't try to take advantage of me, and there won't be any trouble. You do things my way, and it'll all be good."

I could not believe what I was hearing him say: doing things his way; that he was going to be here for months; and that he was stern. There was no way I could learn anything from him. He better not even think about touching me. I was helpless back then, but now I had three inches on him, more weight, and would

punch him in the mouth if he even brought up life back then.

"Okay, I'm going to call roll," he said, starting alphabetically.

I could see girls checking him out, saying he was handsome and cool. If they only knew he was a monster, they would settle down.

Then he got to the *K*s. When he saw my name, he could not even call it out.

"Lan ... don ... K-king?" he said, stuttering over his words. "There's a Landon King in here?"

I immediately jumped up and left the class. I had to get out of there. I could not believe this. I wanted to run outside and scream, but I bumped straight into Ella's twin sister, Eva. She looked frazzled, like she'd been through a lot. Then I remembered what her sister said; I was thinking she needed to go to the bathroom and fix herself up.

I could not worry about her; I had my own issues. So I went into the boys bathroom and kicked the stall. When the bathroom door opened, I abruptly turned. It could not be Mr. Gunn. He did not need to follow me because only one of us would be coming out of this bathroom

alive, and I promise it was not going to be him. I lifted up my fist, ready to pounce on whoever it was.

"Hey, hey, hey," the irritatingly sweet voice called out. "It's me, Carlen. He did something to you too, didn't he?"

"What?" I choked.

Carlen said, "I saw the way you were checking out Gunn. Don't trip. We were on the same team a long time ago. I thought I was the only boy he messed with. The reaction that you just had to seeing him mirrored mine when I stepped into the math class. I was wrong about what I thought before. I was *not* the only one. He messed with you too, didn't he?"

I did not know if I was happy to hear that I was not the only one or what, but I could not confirm Carlen's suspicions. We were nothing alike. Maybe it was all in my mind; after all, Carlen was gay and I was not.

"Just leave me alone, man," I commanded, going out of the bathroom.

Carlen followed me into the hall. "You can't run away from this. He mistreated us, and we can't let him get away with it. He's got to pay."

Throwing up my hands, I kept walking. I was supposed to be in class, but class was the last place I was going. This was hard. I had to remain calm and figure it out. I was not in the fifth grade anymore. For sure, Gunn was not going to win again.

The end of the day could not come fast enough for me. I thought football practice was going to take my mind off my troubles. I really was not into it. Coach was riding me hard.

"King, what's going on, man? You running like a freaking girl," Coach Strong yelled.

And while he had no idea what was going on with me, those words sent me over the edge. On the next play Amir Knight, a defensive back who was faster than lightning, tried to defend me. Angry, I pushed him off something hard.

Leo stood with some of his other defensive teammates and said, "Ooh, Knight, man, you got handled by my boy."

Coach rushed up to me and hit me with a clipboard that was in his hand and yelled, "King, what the heck, man? I can't afford for any of y'all to get injured."

Without realizing who I was talking to, I yelled back, "Well, what the heck, Coach? You said I wasn't giving an effort. I ain't no doggone girl."

"And you gonna get put outta the game if you do something stupid like that on Friday night. Use your head for more than a hat rack."

"Dad, what are you talking about?" Blake called out.

Coach Strong explained, "He needs to think. All of y'all need to think. We got a couple of big games down the stretch. We're undefeated and everybody's gunning for us."

Okay, that word set me off again. Did he have to say *gunning*? Why could he have not said coming for us or trying to knock us off course, ready to beat us, anything, but *gunning* for us? Yeah, I was way too sensitive. I could not keep practicing. I took my helmet off and threw it down on the ground.

Blake quickly picked it up, came over to me, and said, "Man, what's wrong with you? You know my dad's riding us hard with this big game coming up."

"I *need* to go," I uttered, trying to get around my boy.

"We have another hour of practice."

I yelled, "I need to go."

"You better go tell my dad something. You don't need to get mad at the rest of us and let us take heat for whatever is up your tail."

That comment got to me. Gosh, every little thing was reminding me of what Gunn did to me. I was shaking.

When Blake saw I was serious, he said, "I'm just kidding, man. What's up? You all right? You ain't got nobody pregnant have you?"

Actually that would have been a good thing—not really—but at least I would have known my manhood would not be under suspicion. Not that I was questioning it, but just this whole recent turn of events was freaking me out. Coach Strong blew his whistle, and when I looked in his direction, he called me over to the sidelines.

Coach demanded, "What's your problem, King? Talk to me, son. I got progress reports. You got As and Bs. So it can't be that. You're not like your best buddy, Leo Steele, who has problems with his home environment. Unlike Blake, you don't have a dad breathing down your neck. You

got the best one in the world. So what is your problem? I need your head on this field, son."

"Coach, I need to go see my dad. Some stuff is going on, and it's real personal. I'm sorry. If you need to bench me this week, it's cool."

"Nah, I don't need to bench you. I need you to play. Go take care of whatever it is, and then bring your butt out here tomorrow ready to work. Go," Coach Strong ordered. Before I could jog off, he grabbed my collar. "And look, if you need to talk to me about anything, you know you can do that."

"Thanks, Coach," I said.

As quickly as I could, I drove to Lakeside Baptist Church. It was a beautiful building, but in my mind it was the hateful place that took my dad away from me. Yeah, just like Coach Strong said, everybody thought I had it going on and had the best dad in the world. I wished that was the case.

My father had no idea what was troubling me. It was so heavy, so hard, and so tough that he needed to be in on it. I was ecstatic when I pulled up to the pastor's parking space and saw his Benz parked there. I punched in the code

and got into the side entrance of the church. His office door was shut.

Mabel, his personal assistant, a precious lady in her sixties said, "Slow down there, Landon. Your dad's taping. You can't go in there right now, baby."

I wanted to scream at her. "Don't try to stop me. This is important! You don't know what's going on. Get my dad or I'm going in there." But like the good child I had always been, I sat in the waiting room with four other parishioners.

One couple was crying. "Why? Why couldn't this baby live?" the wife cried to her husband. "I just can't do it anymore. I don't want to try for another baby. It just hurts too much."

"We just need to talk to Pastor King. He's going to encourage you," the husband replied.

A lady sitting beside me was rocking back and forth. She had a foreclosure notice and some eviction papers in her hand. She clutched her hands and looked above.

She then looked at me and said, "You're Pastor King's son. I just hope the church can help me. They're going to put me out my house. It's been hard ever since Leroy died."

Another lady was sitting there talking on her cell phone. "If I can just get in there to see Pastor King, he's got to go to bat with the courts for JayBo. I know he shouldn't have robbed those people, but he's a good kid. He can't go to jail. I know Pastor King can help us."

When my dad opened up the door, I wanted to run to him and say, "I need you to hold me. I need you to talk to me. You gotta listen to me. I'm important, please." Feeling for them, I knew there were three other situations more important. They truly needed my dad at the moment. He was their protector, and I had to get out of his way so—to them—he could remain true.

CHAPTER 2

Resist Standing

Well, if it isn't Landon King," the monster Mr. Gunn declared like we were old pals. I had decided to face my enemy and go to math class. "I hope you don't plan to run out of my class this time. Were you sick a couple days ago or what? I didn't even get to say hello."

He held out his hand like I was supposed to shake it or something. I gave him the coldest stare I could, daring him to try me. How could he act like he did nothing? Sitting at my desk, I wondered why he had a smile on his face. It was a sly grin, and I wanted to punch it off of him.

For two days, I wondered what it would be like when I came face to face with him. Would

he act like he did not know me? Would he try to want to get with me? Well, now I had my answer, which was in the middle. He wanted to pretend we were cool. I was young, but I did not forget.

A girlie voice, which was clearly Carlen's, whispered, "If looks could kill, he would be dead. Problem is they don't, so what you gonna do about it? Are you going to let him keep roaming the halls, looking for his next victim? I saw him all yesterday hanging out at the PE class looking at the ninth graders. We can't let him get away with this, Landon. We can't let him molest another boy."

Not even realizing I was engaging Carlen, I said, "You think hanging out with freshmen is something … he's back hanging at the park with the little league football kids."

Carlen hit his desk, raised his hands, and shouted, "See? That's crazy! We gotta do something!"

"Is there a problem back there?" Mr. Gunn asked.

Inside, I wanted to say, "That's a stupid question. You know there's a problem back here. You're looking straight at two of the guys who

you took advantage of years ago. Let's take it to the police. There's a big problem."

For some reason, I resisted and said nothing. The resistance made me angry. Anytime anyone said anything to me all day, I bit their head off. I was mad at the world. It was bad enough this happened to me years ago. Why did this man have to come back into our lives? More than anything, I was angry at myself. Sure, back then he intimidated me into keeping silent. Now I was practically grown. There was absolutely no reason why I could not turn him in.

When I got to football practice, Coach Strong met me and said, "Okay, are you better today?"

I wanted to get smart and say, "Do I look better?" Knowing better, I gave him the answer he wanted to hear and said, "Yes, sir."

Coach was working us hard. Everyone was not giving him one hundred percent, but he was pulling it out of us. He reeled us in for a powwow.

"Listen, men, I'm gonna be real with you guys and talk straight. I know I have been hard on you, and I know you're tired because you have given so much throughout the season, but we're almost at the finish line. There's a big reward waiting

for us. We're trying to get into the playoffs and have home-field advantage. We set ourselves up in a good position so far. Now is not the time to get lazy. Remember, whatever effort you put in is what you are going to get out. You do nothing and nothing is gonna happen. That's why I'm pushing you, 'cause when things get tough in life, you start asking yourself why me? I want you to remember this game of football because it's also the game of life. When trouble comes you can say, 'Why not?' You can take the bull by the horns. You can handle the tough stuff and don't let the tough stuff handle you."

Coach Strong had no idea how much he was speaking to my soul. I needed to hear his talk. Coach Strong's encouragement made me realize that I did need to do something. This whole situation was eating at me, and if I didn't push the shark teeth away, there would be nothing left. Deciding to be bold, I thought that if Carlen had been molested too, maybe he and I weren't the only ones. I suppressed *my* memories and didn't want to talk about them. Maybe there were other guys out there who couldn't deal with the situation either and had never said a word.

Back then, Coach Gunn was the Man in little league football. Tons of young boys went through his care. Maybe that was just it; he didn't care for us at all to be able to mistreat us so bad.

I looked around the football team, and I knew some people weren't even around back then. Blake moved here in ninth grade, which was good because that meant Coach Strong never knew Mr. Gunn. I would hate to think lots of adults knew and covered up this despicable act.

Our great defensive back, Amir, used to play in little league, but I don't think he played in middle school. I started thinking maybe he stopped playing for the same reason I did. My feet jogged over to him, and I smiled because I needed him to forgive me for my rough actions.

"Sorry about pushing you down the other day, man," I said to Amir.

"Nah, it's cool. Just get ready to knock some heads this weekend. I'm straight. For real, though, I didn't know if I had done something to you or what."

"You didn't. Just got a lot on my mind, you know?"

"You wanna talk about it?" Amir asked.

I really appreciated that our team was tight. So many of us were going through so much. Blake's mom had cancer. Leo's mom moved away and left him homeless. ER was waiting for his eligibility, and we tried being there for each other so that the hard things wouldn't keep us down.

"Serious, man. You wanna talk, I'm here."

Needing to clarify the memories in my head, I asked him, "I was just thinking about little league football a long time ago, you know? Weren't we on the same team?"

"Nah, man. I played against you," Amir laughed. "Y'all beat us in the championship."

"Oh, okay. I just thought, you might have been on my team."

"Didn't Leo and Brenton play with you?"

"Yeah, yeah, that's right. They did," I agreed as more memories came flooding back.

Amir called out to both Leo and Brenton. They jogged over. I was not ready to chat, and I did not want to push myself to know.

Quickly, I added, "Oh, I'm straight. We ain't gotta talk about it now. We got practice."

"Talk about what?" Leo asked with a puzzled look on his face.

"Your boy here is having a sentimental moment. He's thinking back to our time in little league football," Amir teased.

"That's probably because our coach is here subbing in math," Brenton offered.

"Yeah, Coach Gunn is here. What did you think about him?" I asked, wondering if Brenton was really connecting with my thoughts.

"He was straight with me," Leo cut in.

Brenton smiled and laughed. "Yeah, I thought he was cool too. We won."

Leo bragged, "Didn't we play you, Amir?"

"Aight, I just went through this with yo' ole teammate here. He thought I played with y'all." Amir shook his head.

"Nah, Landon, we beat him," Leo said.

Wanting to be clear about my teammates and their feelings toward Coach Gunn, I asked, "So, Brenton, Leo, y'all liked him?"

"Why would we not?" Leo asked me.

Brenton squinted "You didn't?"

At that moment, Coach Strong blew his whistle three times real hard. "Listen, boys, we don't have time for a gossip session. Let's go, gentlemen, we got work to do."

I was happy we had to disperse. The tough guys I knew who were under Coach Gunn's care had not been affected. I saw Leo looking over at me, and I looked away and started following instructions from Coach Strong. Again, I suppressed the urge to tell all.

Brenton and Leo were two guys I respected. If they thought Gunn was upstanding, cool. Maybe I needed to drop the whole thing. Who was going to believe me and Carlen? If this got out, people could think I was just like him, fruity and soft. Shoot, I was going to keep my mouth shut. I had too much to lose.

When practice was over, I saw Leo waiting around for Coach Strong. My friend looked anxious and slightly upset. I noticed Leo was pacing. Had he lied to me? Was he going through the same experiences I was? Did Coach Gunn cross the line with him long ago? I had to know.

I went over to him and said, "What's up, man? I can take you home."

"Nah, I'll wait on Coach Strong."

Leo was staying at the Strong's home, and I hadn't seen him much lately. I missed hanging

with him. He usually rode with Blake, but Blake was already gone.

"I can't believe your boy didn't even wait on you," I said to Leo, noticing he still looked uneasy.

"Nah, it's cool. He's gonna pick his mom up from her treatment," Leo said, looking like I was bothering him. "Go ahead, Landon, I'm straight, man."

"Please, I want to talk to you," I said, being honest and bold.

At that moment, Coach Strong came out of the office. Leo looked relieved until Coach spoke. "Leo, why don't you catch a ride with Landon. I need to study some film with the coaches. It's gonna take a while. Go ahead. I know you want to get to your mom."

At that moment, Leo's eyes opened wide. I knew I heard Coach Strong right. He mentioned Leo's mom. Was she back? If so, that was good news. Why hadn't Leo told me? I grabbed his bag and dashed out of the locker room. He had to follow me to get it. I got in the car and unlocked the other side. He reluctantly got in.

He shut the door with a frown on his face. "Okay, you're tripping," I announced. "Your

mom's got you that upset? She's back, man. This is a good thing. Is that dude with her?"

I actually wouldn't mind giving Leo's mom a good talking to. There was no way I could forgive her for leaving him to fend for himself like she did, following someone she barely knew to go to New York for a chance to start over. That boy had been through a lot in the last couple of weeks: beat up, practically left for dead, and shot at. He turned out okay and even made it through the shooting. His girlfriend got hit with the bullet instead, but she was okay. Now his mom was back. What was the story?

"Are you mad at your mom or something? Did the guy threaten you? Is it something with the Axes?"

The Axes was the local gang. They were behind most of the area's violence. Many of them were arrested after the shooting, including the ringleader, Shameek.

"Have you heard from any of them?" Leo spoke up and asked.

"Word's out they are tryin' to recruit." Leo looked at me like I better not try and join them.

Showing him I had not lost my mind, I said, "Nah, I'm not even thinking about any of that."

"Turn here," Leo said to me when he was satisfied I wasn't turning gangster.

"Where you taking me, man? It's too far out of the way. I know the shortcut to get to Blake's place."

"I'm not going to Blake's," Leo said harshly.

"Quit being evasive. Talk to a brother."

"I'm not the only one who's acting weird, so don't even put any pressure on me to be real. You don't even have to take me far; you can just drop me off. I can walk to where I need to go."

"I don't understand, Leo," I said. Why was he pulling away? "I got a car, and I can take you wherever you need to go. I just need to know what's going on with you. You gonna answer any of my questions about your mom? When did she get back? And why aren't you excited about it?"

"I feel you, man. Just take me to the corner. I got a lot of heavy stuff laying on me, okay? You wouldn't understand," Leo confessed with a heavy heart. It seemed like four hundred pounds was weighing on his chest.

"Okay, you already just said I was trippin'. I got some substantial stuff weighing on me too, but aren't we supposed to be there for each other, brother? Can't we talk about stuff?"

"Are you ready to open up to me?"

"Yes," I uttered honestly, knowing that meant I was ready to talk about my pain.

"Not that I believe you have any drama. Your life is perfect. Daddy Rich always takes care of you," Leo sneered.

"Okay," I snapped back. I hastily pulled the car into McDonald's. "You talk to me, and I talk to you."

"You want me to go first, right?" Leo asked with resignation.

"I'm the one with the car. Besides, you gotta trust me. You first, then me. But don't belittle me and assume I ain't got no worries. Money is not the only thing that can mess a brother up. Now talk."

After a long pause, Leo said, "All right, here it goes. I'm happy my mom's back. She said she made a mistake. It really bums me out that she's going through so much, but she's back. She just ain't got nothing—not a dollar or pot to her name."

"She's got you," I belted out, needing him to get that love was important.

"Exactly, so I'm not even staying with the Strongs anymore. I'm over there with her."

"Okay, good," I said. "So where's 'over there?' "

"We're staying in a homeless shelter. It is the smallest feeling a man can have. I promise you that I'm down to get my education and go on to college. I've got to make something of my life. I really wanna make a go at so much. I'm not just dreaming of getting into the NFL. Though I know it's where I belong, I plan to have options."

"Man, you're good, though."

"Thanks. I got a shot at getting there. You talking about somebody motivated. Living on the streets has shown me that I'm certainly not going to get it my own way. Bring on the hard curriculum. Bring on the crucial workouts. I need a D1 scholarship. I can't live like this."

Leo put his head in his hands. He let out sobs. I hated seeing him breaking.

I began encouraging him. "You know you are a man."

"Please, dude, I ain't got nothing to offer my mom," Leo cried.

"You're still in school, man. You are making her proud, and you are by her side. Can't nobody mess with her 'cause you're there every night."

"She's working hard at her new job and saving money," Leo said. I could see him trying to compose himself.

"Good. Where is the shelter? I'm dropping you off straight there."

"Thanks, man," Leo said, knowing that he couldn't resist the offer.

It was dark. He didn't need to be walking downtown alone. Though he was a big dude and didn't have a dime in his pocket, people could still jump him because he looked clean cut. No need in being at the wrong place when he did not have to.

When we got down to the shelter, he wouldn't get out. "Wassup?" I asked.

"Remember we had a deal, Landon King. What's going on with you?"

"I'm straight, man. I'm straight," I said, knowing my friend already had a bunch on his plate. I did not want to topple it by adding on my problems.

"C'mon, dude, don't give me that."

When Leo would not relent, I said, "All right, all right. I was asking you earlier about little league and being on Coach Gunn's team."

"Yeah, and what about it?"

"It was the things he did to me, man, when we were little that I never told you about."

"What? What are you saying?" Leo asked me, and I saw anger rise in his eyes.

"Yeah, man, all that you think plus. I just want to forget it ever happened."

As if he remembered something, he cut me off and said, "You did get a little weird back then. You never came to the banquet to get your trophy, but you didn't tell anybody why."

"Never thought I had to see him again, but now he's back, man."

"How we gonna deal with it?" Leo asked.

That made me smile. He was a good brother. I put my hands on the steering wheel and gave a heavy sigh. How *was* I gonna deal with it? Now at least I knew I wouldn't have to go through it alone. My boy was gonna help me figure it out. Help me stand.

"You know you straight, right?" Leo said, awakening my concerns.

"Heck yeah, I'm straight," I said, thinking he meant straight, like not gay.

"No, I mean, like you're cool? He took advantage. This wasn't none of your fault. Don't carry this, man. Like you just told me about my mom, some stuff is out of our control, and other people's choices affect us, but it's not gonna kill us."

"Yeah, you're right. I'm straight," I agreed. We gave each other dap before he got out of the car. I was relieved I'd shared my past, but I was now uneasy about the future.

The talk with Leo helped me to feel stronger. I was a victim, yes. Gunn wasn't gonna break me, though.

Getting dressed for his football game, Logan remarked, "Mom, Landon has been acting really weird. I don't want him to take me anymore," my brother said emphatically.

"He's not taking you there, Logan. I am taking you to the game. He's just picking you up, sweetie. You know Mom and Dad have so much running around to do." I could not see Logan's face, but he must not have thought she was really going

to be busy. Our mom continued to convince him. “Thanksgiving’s coming up, and we’re having this drive for the homeless. The women’s ministry is sponsoring it, sweetie. I’m going to be there for the first quarter of your game, but your brother is coming, and he will be there at the end.”

I walked into the kitchen. I was happy to eat the scones the chef prepared. That was one of the luxuries of having loaded parents. We had a staff at our beck and call to make our household run smoothly.

“I can have Mr. Grady pick you up, Logan, but I thought you wanted Landon to be there.”

My little brother looked away. He didn’t want me to see his disappointment. I’d already heard, though.

“No need to be turning around now, Log,” I said to my little brother. I used his pet name to get him to lighten up. “I heard you.”

“What are you doing to him, Landon? Your brother doesn’t want you at the game?” My mother came up to me and tugged on my arm.

Logan uttered, “I want him there, Mom. It’s just he’s been acting weird the last two times that he came. He’s like a stalker or something.”

My mom said, “Now, Landon, you know you can’t get so involved in this football stuff. It’s only pee-wee level football. Don’t put any pressure on your little brother.”

“No, Mom, he knows we know how to ball,” Logan explained, “but it’s like Landon thinks I’m gonna break every time we’re alone with the coaches. He comes rushing out there like he wants to be the only one who tells me what to do or something.”

“Why is that, sweetheart?” my mom asked me in a caring tone, having no clue of all I endured back then.

I wanted to say “I don’t know, Mom … Why is that? Shouldn’t you know? It’s good to collect canned goods for the homeless. Same drive you used to do back when I was playing ball, but you got some hungry sons in front of you, longing for and needing attention, hungry for your love, wanting to be put first just once.” Honestly, I was so disgusted I couldn’t even think.

“Hurry up and go get dressed, Logan,” my mom ordered. It seemed like her time became more important than getting to the bottom of what was ailing me.

I huffed. When she saw that I was frustrated, she pulled out two chairs. I thought that maybe I was important after all.

"Okay, son, sit," she told me. Then she looked at her watch again.

"I'm fine, Mom," I said. I wanted to stand.

"What's going on with you, Landon? Why are you so uptight, son?"

It took everything in me not to just let it all out and give her a true piece of my mind. However, I had a year and a half left and then I'd be gone. I could count on my hand how many times she'd been to any of my extracurricular activities. Unfortunately, she was doing the exact same thing to my brother. Why did my parents give so much to the world and just give us their leftover time—when they had any? While I did have many luxuries given to me by my parents, I would trade it all in for more of their time.

I took Tae Kwon Do classes to help me with flexibility, concentration, and stamina while going through football training. When training with the punching bag, I always had a vision of Gunn in my mind. I wanted to kick him. Punch

him. Scream in his face and knock him to the ground. I took it all out on the punching bag, because I wasn't a killer. Any thought of really doing that to him was out, even though, like his last name, he had shot my life to a gloomy, dark place. I had to help make Mr. Gunn set it right.

Normally, after Tae Kwon Do I headed over to the mall, got an outfit or two, went to the food court, flirted with some chicks, and called my boys to see who was getting into what. Today, I needed to get over to the park just in case my mom wasn't looking. After all, she didn't know what to be watching out for. If something were to happen to my brother, I couldn't live with myself. I told Coach Brown that Mr. Gunn did not need to be anywhere around other kids, but I didn't give an explanation as to why. Therefore, why should I think he obliged my request?

When I got there, I looked for my mom. She was gone. That didn't surprise me. I could only hope since the game was going on that Logan did not have time to be alone with any coach.

She texted me and said, "Logan's having a great game. Please support him and give him some space. Love, Mom."

My mom was right. The little quarterback had a great arm. When I walked up, Logan caught a thirty-yard pass and ran in for a touchdown. When the team was on defense, Logan played the defensive back position, and on the first play I saw, he caught an interception. Then the offense was back on the field. I couldn't stay in my seat. I was yelling and cheering and extremely proud of my little brother.

When the game was over, I dashed over to my brother and lifted him up in the air.

"You're the man, Logan. You're a leader on the team, flying in the air like you're leaping to your throne, catching balls left and right, and holding it down. That was tight."

"You like my game, for real? I told you I can ball. I learned so much from you." Logan beamed and radiated happiness.

Then I heard some yelling. I turned around and saw Coach Brown arguing with Mr. Gunn. Throughout the game, I had been looking for the guy, but I hadn't seen him until now.

"I'm gonna say something to my quarterback," Logan said, which was fine because I wanted to hear what was going on.

"Just don't leave this field," I instructed my brother.

I walked over to the sidelines. As I got closer, I could hear the two of them going at it. Thankfully, no other parents were watching.

Coach Brown said, "I just asked you not to come out here anymore. I don't know why you can't abide by that. I don't need to go through this. I got my reasons."

"I mean, if you not telling me why, then what's the big deal? Shoot, I didn't think you were serious. So you been winning a couple of games; you want to have seasons like I had. That's your legacy out here, and you don't need to be so proper that you can't accept my help," Mr. Gunn said. "You can't tell me not to show up at a public park."

"Look, man, I don't want no trouble," Coach Brown declared. "I just asked you not to come out here."

"Is there a problem?" I asked.

Coach Gunn looked at me like he wanted to take a steel bat and knock my head off, but I wasn't a little boy. I had manned up. I was ready for him to try me.

"Is there a problem?" I said a little louder.

"Just go on, Landon, I got this," Coach Brown said, clearly not wanting to pull me in.

"What have you been saying to him?" Mr. Gunn confronted me face to face.

"He didn't tell me anything. It was my decision to ask that you not come around, okay? Do I need to call the police?" Coach Brown threatened. Mr. Gunn would not stop staring at me.

"Oh, it's like that? Fine, fine, I don't wanna be around your stupid program anyway," Mr. Gunn yelled before storming off.

When I saw Mr. Gunn get into his car and speed off, I turned back to my brother's coach. Coach Brown was waiting for something. I squinted, unsure of what that was.

"Is there something you need to say to me? Is there something you wanna talk about?" he inquired.

I didn't want to respond. I had a rep to protect. As bad as all the memories were for me, I had to keep quiet and resist standing.

CHAPTER 3

Must Choose

Hey, Landon, you can't avoid me anymore. I've been calling you and calling you, and you haven't called me back," Carlen said. Then he came up behind me and tried to tickle me.

"Man, what are you doing?" I stammered, almost losing it.

"Dang, I'm just playing. Ease up. I'm not trying to get into your pants." But all of the hundreds of pairs of eyes on me thought so. "Look, don't be so sensitive," Carlen said, lowering his voice because he realized I was uncomfortable with his gestures. "Plus you're not my type anyway."

I wanted to punch him. When I tried to walk away from Carlen, he followed me toward

my class. Thankfully, this was not the day I had to deal with Gunn, but with Carlen as a gnat I wanted to swat, I was just as agitated.

Waxton pushed me into Carlen and said, "Dang, King, I didn't know you had your own special cheerleader."

"You wish I did cartwheels for you, baby," Carlen called out to the big man in our school.

Once the hall was empty, I took his arm and dug my fingers into it real hard and pulled him over to an isolated corner. Of course, I was looking all around making sure no one saw me do that, because then people would think all kinds of things. I was excessively paranoid not wanting that to happen.

"Okay, okay, I can tell you're uncomfortable around me. Like being gay is a disease you can catch or something," Carlen stated.

I lashed out, "What do you want, Carlen? I saw your calls. You should've been able to get the message when I didn't return them. What's up?"

"It's this thing with Gunn. I'm going to the police."

"What?" I uttered, more shocked than if my father announced he was leaving the pulpit.

This issue was dead. There was no need to stir it up. Carlen needed to chill and know I wasn't feeling his idea.

"Yeah, and you need to go with me. We can go tell Dr. Sapp. Maybe he'll call the police up to the school, and they can hear both our stories. When we tell them what happened—"

Cutting him off, I said, "Wait, wait, wait, don't make any plans for me. If that's what you want to do, I can't stop you. Don't put my name anywhere in it."

"I've wanted to tell them everything that happened so they don't just think it's me. I've been thinking about this, and whether you go with me or not, I'm telling all I know … including what I know about you. If you get on the stand and you lie, that's perjury. And lying can do a lot of damage. All that stress could affect the way you handle the pressure of school and football. No one wants a loose cannon on their team. As a pastor's son, you have a moral obligation. People expect you to tell the truth."

By not saying anything for the last five and a half years, I had gotten pretty good at lying to myself about what happened. I told myself

that it did not happen so much that I started to believe it. It was my choice whether or not I changed that and told all, not Carlen's.

Trying to appeal to a person so determined to right the world, I said, "Look, I'm sorry this happened to you. Hey, it happened to me too, but it's my business. I'm asking you man to man or man to whatever it is that you want to be called."

"I'm a man, don't trip," he said in his irritating, feminine voice.

"Great, well then, I'm asking you to let this be. Particularly when it comes to me."

Suddenly, Carlen got some guts and pushed me. I was not as muscular as Leo and Brenton, but I could snap the boy if I wanted. So I threw my hands up in the air and stepped back.

I said, "Be mad all you want, man, but I ain't saying nothing."

"I got more backbone than you, Landon King." He tried to act all tough. "Because when it comes to standing up for something and not being such a selfish prick, you take the easy way out and hide."

"I don't expect you to understand my reasons. Heck, all of this just came back up a couple

of days ago. I'm still wrestling with it around in my head myself, but for now, this is my decision. So please just leave me alone." I walked away.

Carlen ran up behind me and touched my waist. "Please, wait."

I looked back at him with eyes that could shoot daggers.

Leo came up and asked, "Is there a problem here?"

"Hey, Leo," Carlen said, getting his flirt on. "I got a problem; my back is itching. Can you scratch it?" Leo frowned at the flirting girlie-boy. Carlen clearly let me know Leo was his type. "Oh, you can't. You did choose Miss Ella. I should've sabotaged her behind in in-school suspension last month. Dang it, I let a good one get away. Bye, King, acting like a queen," Carlen claimed, sashaying away.

"What's up, man?" Leo laughed. "Why is he sweating you?"

After being hesitant, I said, "He played on our little league team too."

"Yeah, I remember."

"Everything that happened to me wasn't an isolated incident."

Leo placed a brief empathetic touch on my shoulder. “Dang, what? Word.”

“Yeah, happened to him too,” I repeated.

“He used to be different back then. Like one of us, tough and stuff.”

“I know, man. I don’t know if it made him gay, but it made me want to get with the girls over and over and over, like it was some stupid addiction or something. It affected us both, and he wants to tell.”

“I think y’all should, man. The fool is back acting like he has never done anything to anybody. You can’t just let him get away with that.”

“Easy for you to say. It’s honorable that you are helping your mom out, staying with her at the homeless shelter instead of at Coach Strong’s, but you don’t want anybody to know. What happened to me wasn’t honorable at all, and if they put me in the same category as Carlen, I’m going to be called everything from fag to homo to who knows what else.”

“Please, you don’t have to worry about that. You know what you are,” Leo said to me. “There’s too many honeys around here who will line up and vouch that you got a man card.”

"Yeah, but I have never really been able to fall for none of them. You know, like this feeling you have with Ella."

"What? So you think just because you're not in love you're gay?"

"Watch it now," I threatened.

"I'm just saying, man, as crazy as that sounds to you is as crazy as it sounds to me. Don't get the facts twisted and don't let Gunn off the hook because you're afraid of what others might think if they found out. Screw them. Uh, I mean figuratively, you know." I nodded. "How are you going to feel if Gunn does this to somebody else, and you didn't do anything? Wouldn't living with the fact that he molested another kid be way worse than some rumors that will blow over in a week or two?"

My soul knew the answer was yes, but my prideful mind was still saying no. Ella came up and grabbed Leo's hand. He kissed her hand and turned to walk her to class. Before he did, he told me that we would finish the talk later. But I did not want to finish this talk with anybody. I wanted this talk to be dead over with and never be brought up again.

ER caught up with me and said, "What's up, King?"

"ER, hey, man. When are you going to get eligible?" I asked.

"Yeah, that's the million-dollar question everyone keeps asking me. You would think that my dad would have had all that stuff figured out before he had me change schools."

"Well, we certainly need you. Our kicker can kick everything but the football."

"Yeah, he kicks the grass, the turf, the dirt, but not the pigskin. Shoot, he misses that every time," ER joked.

"White boys can't jump, and black boys can't kick. That's what they say."

"Well, they're wrong," ER blurted out. "I really came here to play basketball."

"Oh, so you ball too?" I asked. I was impressed at the thought because Leo, Blake, and I were b-ballers too.

"Yeah, tryouts are coming up soon."

"I hope we go far in the playoffs, but for now, I just hope that I'll make the team," I said to him. "There's stiff competition with only five starting spots, so you gotta bring it."

ER looked at me like I didn't know who he was. "No worries there."

"All right, we'll see," I joked. "Like your confidence, though."

ER went left field on me. "Look, I know it's none of my business, but I saw you earlier with Carlen. You seemed uncomfortable. Just because you hang out with a guy who's gay doesn't make you a faggot."

"What do you know about it?" I stepped away.

"Back at my old school, everyone who is gay is out, girls and guys. We've grown up with each other since elementary, so we're still tight. I just wanted to tell you if somebody's your friend, don't let who they like to get with keep you from being their buddy."

I did not know why ER said that to me, but I actually appreciated it. I just had to decide if I wanted to fool with Carlen. I needed to figure out if coming forward was worth it, and I needed to do that before he decided for me.

"Leo Steele, you've grown up into a fine young man. You are making me proud," Mr. Gunn

declared the next day. He had the nerve to try and give my boy dap.

Leo turned his hand into a fist. “Step back, man. I’m just trying to get into the classroom. Don’t be touching on me.”

“Touching on you? What’s the problem? I’m just trying to give you some credit for doing so well this year.”

“I don’t need you to be on my bandwagon, Mr. Gunn,” Leo said coldly.

I was walking right behind him. Mr. Gunn put his hand out so I could not walk into the classroom. He glared at me with blazing fire in his eyes.

Blocking my way, he said, “What have you been telling people? Coach Brown didn’t want me at football. Now Leo doesn’t want me to speak to him. Have you been spreading lies about me?”

“Move your hand,” I said, trying to stay calm.

“Answer the question, Landon,” Mr. Gunn demanded.

I noticed Dr. Sapp was coming down the hall, but he was walking in the direction that Mr. Gunn could not see. So I yelled out, “Hey, Dr. Sapp, can I see you for a second, sir?”

Quickly, Mr. Gunn put down his hand, looked over his shoulder, placed his arm around my shoulder, and said, "Why, hello, Dr. Sapp."

I took Mr. Gunn's arm quickly off my shoulder. "Don't ever tough me again," I hissed.

Dr. Sapp looked perplexed. "Is there a problem here?"

"No, sir, no problem," Mr. Gunn replied.

The principal sensed the tension between Mr. Gunn and myself. "Landon, you were the one who called me, son. What's going on?"

Keeping my cool, I said, "Just wanted to make sure that we can still come to you, you know, if we ever needed to report something."

Dr. Sapp said, "Landon, that goes without saying. Now get in there and learn something, boy. And, Mr. Gunn, don't block the door, man. The students need to get on in the classroom."

"Oh right, right, sir. Sorry about that," Mr. Gunn replied like a wimp.

"That's fine; just don't let it happen again. Kids don't need any excuse for not being able to get into a class."

When Dr. Sapp left, Mr. Gunn came up to me and threatened, "I don't know what kind of

games you're playing, but you're messing with a grown man."

"And you're not messing with a kid anymore," I defended.

Settling his tough tone, he said, "Look, Landon, if there's something you need to say to me, then you just need to talk to me. Say it or just drop it."

"Why are you back here?"

"What kind of question is that?"

"You know what? Forget it. You should've just stayed gone."

"I don't know why you're so hostile. You and I had a good time together, and now you're giving me all this attitude. Like I did something to you, like—"

"You know what? Save it," I said.

I did not even want him trying to lie his way out of the truth. I sat down in my seat, hating with every fast heartbeat that I had to sit in his presence. To me, this was every bit the same kind of treatment a soldier caught behind enemy lines would experience. It was torture.

We got to work in pairs to do the class assignment. Leo paired up with Carlen, and I was

teamed with ER, but I couldn't stop myself from staring at Mr. Gunn with eyes that wanted to destroy him.

"Hey, man," ER finally said. "What's up with you and that teacher? Something's going on, I know that. Look, I know you don't know me that well, but if you need to get something off your chest, I'm here for you."

"I don't need to talk," I snapped as I cut my eyes over at him.

As we started working on the equations, ER just started babbling. "I'll never forget … my best friend in elementary school was molested by our karate instructor. He took him to all of these matches and meets so the kid could compete against boys in other towns. On some of those trips, they shared a room, and that is when the guy invaded my friend's space."

At that moment, it felt like steam was coming out of my ears. I did not know what made ER say all of that to me. He was right on, and it was scary. The only thing I could do was grab him quickly by the collar and yank him over the desk. Everyone in the classroom, including Mr. Gunn, looked our way.

Then ER whispered, “I got to be on your street because if I wasn’t, it wouldn’t have affected you like that.”

“Landon, what are you doing?” Mr. Gunn asked, approaching me and touching my arm.

That was really what I wanted, because I tried to start punching the teacher. ER got up and pulled me away. Leo helped.

“He’s not worth it, man. Just get up and go,” ER said, pushing me through the door.

“I can’t do this. I can’t come back in this class anymore.”

Mr. Gunn charged up behind me. “That’s right, Mr. King,” he said. “You fought with a fellow student and then tried to come after me. You’re going to the principal’s office. I’m gonna get you expelled. ”

I howled back like a wolf ready to open his throat. “Send me to the office, man! You heard Dr. Sapp. I can tell him anything. I can tell on anybody.”

Mr. Gunn tried to get Leo to sit down. That was crazy because now Leo was trying to fight the man. I grabbed Leo and pulled him out into the hallway.

"The three of you guys, out now. Get out!" Mr. Gunn yelled. Just then the bell rang.

I looked over at Leo and ER and said, "Look, sorry I fronted on you. I don't want you guys getting in this. This is my fight."

"If that man did something to you, you can't let him get away with it," ER stated.

Impulsively, I took my hand and squeezed it around his neck real hard. I was so angry. Leo came and took it off.

"Don't get mad at him, man," Leo said. I nodded, and then he turned to ER and asked, "ER, how'd you know, man? How'd you know?"

"I saw him shooting daggers at the sub and I suspected. When I told him I had a friend who got molested by a coach, he freaked on me. That's when I knew I was right."

I wanted to yell out, "I wasn't molested, okay? Drop this. I'm strong; he didn't do anything to me." But I could not say any of that. I just hit the locker and took my book bag and flung it down the hall.

ER walked over to me and said, "Are you just going to let this get the best of you? Are you going to let this man win?"

"I can't have people thinking I'm a punk, man," I ranted. I went over to Leo and said, "People can't think I'm soft. I'm not like Carlen."

"Who are you trying to prove this to, man? People who know you, *know* you. And the ones who don't ... who cares what they think? Since when did you care anyway? You've always been your own man. This dude shouldn't be in our school," Leo said.

I settled down as I walked to class. Then that disturbing voice caught up to me and said, "I don't know what you think you remember about me, or what's getting under your skin, but you can't prove anything. So you need to just drop this, lose the attitude, and let's just figure out a way to get along."

Before I could respond, the voice stopped speaking. I turned and Mr. Gunn was nowhere in sight. Had he actually said something to me or was I truly losing it? Could I prove any of this if I even decided to rat him out? I felt like someone had me by the throat, choking the life out of me. I could not breathe. I could not think. I just kept telling myself I was strong, all the while I felt weak. I could not go on like this. The

problem was that I did not know what I was going to do about it.

Everybody on the football team wanted Brick Bailey, our kicker, to crawl under a rock and stay there. He was not just a bad kicker; he was horrible. Though he was better than the rest of us, being better was still not getting the job done.

We were coming up on the last few games of the season. Brick had only made two of eight field goals thus far, and we all had to hold our breath when it came to his kicking for extra points. It was torture watching ER Stone, our kicking savior, do so well in practice but be unable to compete in the games. Coach and ER's dad were keeping the specifics under wraps. Most of us had heard the problem had something to do with his old high school coach calling the Georgia High School Association and alerting them to the fact that ER was living out of district with a non-custodial parent.

So far, ER was all right, but even though he'd been around for a while, we were still surprised to see him walking in the halls because he had a different skin color.

It was almost the end of the season, and ER could have been green, and it would not have made a difference. We badly needed him to play. Guys were so desperate, things were becoming tense at practices. Waxton went over to Brick and whacked him upside the back of his head.

Wax said, "Dude, this is my senior year. So far the kicking hasn't cost us any games, but it's only a matter of time. I want a championship. So you need to do whatever it is that you need to do to get control of your freaking foot."

"Or what?" Brick threatened, pushing Wax.

Waxton yelled, "Word's out that you've been giving half effort, jealous because we're in ER's camp now."

Brick said, "And how is that working out for y'all? He can't even play. So you need to step up out of my face and let me practice."

"Is practicing gonna help you?" Waxton asked condescendingly.

"Is a peppermint going to help your bad breath?" Brick yelled, and the players around him laughed at Wax.

The only thing I had going in my life right now was the Lockwood Lions. Leo, Blake, and

Amir felt the same way. To win the state title as a junior would ensure that we'd become blue-chip players in the eyes of top college scouts. As more guys started to laugh at Waxton, he took all that anger and hostility and stormed over to ER, who was not even near the broiling brawl.

ER was kicking the ball from the thirty yard line with the long snapper. As soon as the ball went through the uprights, the two players slapped each other's hands. Waxton had reached ER by then and tackled him to the ground. Nothing like this had happened at practice in a while. What craziness was going to happen next? Coaches were inside going over practice plans. We were supposed to be warming up, yet the entire crowd left Brick and rushed over to the thirty yard line to see the two of them wrestling, as if that was their sport rather than football.

"You come out here thinking you're better than us, rubbing our nose all in the fact that you can kick, yet in games you're insignificant. Brick needs to be the one over here working the uprights."

"We have two end zones," ER said. "Get off of me, and get out of my face."

Waxton would not let go of ER's practice jersey. I would not say ER was my friend, but other than us going at it today, we were definitely cool. When I needed someone to have my back and keep me straight, he was there giving even unsolicited advice. It was my turn to do the same for him. I gave Leo a look like, *All right, let's get involved and squash this drama*. I grabbed ER, and Leo grabbed Waxton.

"Wax, why all of a sudden are you acting like the hoodlum that my friends at my old school say you are?" ER said. I knew right away that wasn't gonna go over well with my teammates.

In truth, ER might've had a great point. Waxton did flex his muscles too much. Every time you turned around, he was intimidating somebody with bullying tactics. However, hearing any white boy say that any one of us was thuggish people at Lockwood got us hot under the collar.

I got in front of ER's face and said, "Look, you don't want to make this a race thing."

"Please, he's the one saying I think I'm better than you guys. What else was he referring to? It ain't like I got a wad of money coming

out of my butt, so he couldn't have been talking about my finances. He's talking about my skin color, Landon, and I'm not apologizing because I'm white."

"Why'd you leave your other school?" Blake questioned. "Your old coach sure has it out for my dad, calling him out to the Georgia High School Association, saying that he went and recruited you on his own."

ER defended, "Your dad knows that's not true."

"So black people know we're not inferior to whites, but that doesn't mean the people over at your old school don't think otherwise. If you're going to play on the team, then you need to play on the team," Blake stated.

One player yelled out. "Yeah, do we need to go over to your old school and shake things up? Scare them into dropping the allegations and leaving Coach alone?"

"Proving their theory about folks over here at this school?" ER turned and said to whoever opened his mouth.

"That we are what? Gangsters? Ghetto? Stupid?" Waxton yelled.

"All right, guys, let's just drop all of the tension," I ordered. I put my hands on ER's chest while the masses were crowding in on us. "Ever since he's been on this team, he's had the same practices we've had. Even though he's not a skilled position player and a lot of things we get disciplined for have nothing to do with him, he still takes the punishment with us; he's been a team player. Any of y'all got beef with him, take it up with me. He'll be eligible soon, and he doesn't need to be hurt so he can't play when that happens. Go on, y'all, go on!" I yelled.

Waxton was the last one to leave. It was as if he just couldn't let go of the anger he had built up. Leo and Blake pulled him away.

"When do you think you're going to get eligible?" I asked ER.

I thought I was doing something that would help diffuse the situation. If ER gave me some idea about his eligibility, I could relay it to everyone, and folks could chill. Things were getting way out of control. I wondered that maybe if ER gave a little coaching help to the kicker we *did* have, then maybe some of the hostility would dissipate.

He stepped to my face real tight and said, "Look, you might think you did me a favor coming over here looking all big and bad, like I need you to take up for me. Please, you can't even handle your own situation. I got this. I'm not scared of anyone on this team. I'm not a punk. I might be white; that's obvious, but my tough demeanor is not. If any of them want to try me to find out, I'm fine with that."

"You're the one who needs to check yourself. I already know what's going on with you. You know, you assume you know—"

"No, I know. Carlen talked to me."

"What?" I shouted. I couldn't believe what I was hearing. I wished Carlen was out here so I could pound his face.

"You want to help somebody out and do the right thing? Turn in Mr. Gunn. Just because you can stand up, don't think you're doing me a favor. You think you're all big and bad. Then decide, your reputation or true honor. I don't need you to stick up for me. You really think you're a man with balls? Then figure out what's most important to you. Take a real stand, because you can't straddle the fence. You must choose."

CHAPTER 4

Unthinkable Guilt

Sitting in the stands early Saturday morning and watching my little brother play another dominant little league football game, I felt uncomfortable. I should have been extremely happy that Logan was doing his thing. On offense, he caught two short passes and ran them several yards for touchdowns. On defense, because he was tall, they had him playing defensive end, and he had three sacks on the other team's poor quarterback.

Yeah, my chest should have been sticking out way far. I was good in little league, but I wasn't the most valuable player. It was clear that the quarterback, running back, linebacker,

and defensive back were helping this team lead their region. But mostly it was all Logan King. Though I was proud of my brother, I was still inwardly struggling. I couldn't really even enjoy the game.

My eyes searched the bushes, the parking lot, the stands, and everywhere in between for Mr. Gunn. He wasn't happy when he was told to leave at the last game, and I hadn't forgotten his cold, red eyes that glared at me with hatred. Though I hadn't confessed a thing to him, I was certain he had no doubts that I remembered.

If anything happen to Logan, and I didn't say anything because I wanted to protect my own interests, I would be devastated. Honestly, as tough as I was, I didn't know if I would be able to live with myself if harm was brought to my brother or anyone else. The thought of another boy being held against his will and forced to participate made me literally throw up the sausage, egg, and cheese biscuit I had just put into my stomach.

"Oh my gosh, young man, are you okay?" one of the mothers in the stands asked.

Her husband joked, "Obviously, he isn't okay. He just threw up all over the place. Get him some napkins or something."

"Good thing the game's almost over," another parent shouted.

I clutched my chest and tried hard to catch my breath. These feelings of guilt were consuming me. My mind flashed an image of Mr. Gunn at the elementary school in his car, scouting his next victim. When the teacher turned her back on the playground and a boy went to pick up a runaway ball, I envisioned Gunn scooping up the kid. Then the orange juice I just had came up.

People fled from the stands. I didn't blame them. I actually hated that I was causing such an uproar. All of this was Gunn's fault. Why didn't I have the guts to make him pay?

The mom who had spoken to me earlier handed me a bottle of water. "Here, sweetie, drink this," she said.

"Thank you," I gasped.

I tried sipping on the water, but I was getting choked up as I thought about the same little boy who I imagined being taken from the

playground—dead. Had he committed suicide? Had Gunn murdered him? Either way it didn't matter. All of this could have been avoided if I would have just stood up, but I couldn't. Wheezy, I dropped to my knees, putting my hands in my vomit to try and brace myself so that I wouldn't hit my head on the bleachers. People were hitting me on my back, thinking that I was choking and losing my air flow.

Finally, after a few scary moments of feeling like my life was being sucked away, I said, "I'm okay."

I looked up. I probably had ten parents around me. A couple refs and Coach Brown made sure I was okay too.

I could hear my brother, Logan, yelling, "He's my brother. I need to see if he's okay. Please let me make sure he's all right!"

"I'm okay, Logan," I said, trying to get myself together. "Tell Logan I'm fine."

"The paramedics are sitting just around the corner on stand-by since we are playing games all day. Do I need to call someone for you?" Coach Brown asked.

"I'm fine, sir," I replied.

"I got your mom's number right here. I'll call her and let her know what's going on," Coach Brown stated.

But I raised my hand to stop him, and in a stern voice I protested, "Sir, I said I was okay. I'm not ill. I'm not sick. Just got a little queasy in my stomach, but I'm find now. I probably just ate too fast."

The silly husband from earlier said, "That's food poisoning. I told my wife you can't just go to any ole kind of restaurant. You gotta check that stuff. It's salmonella. It's salmanicky. It's salmawemo. It's something."

"You had it right the first time, dear," she declared. Everyone laughed at the change of mood.

There were only two minutes left in the game. When Coach Brown felt I was okay, they all went back over to the field and continued playing, though no one could sit in the stands. There were only a few bleachers, and I pretty much sprayed all of them with the contents of my stomach.

I heard people whispering, "Doesn't he play for the Lions?"

"Yeah, Lockwood's got a big game tonight."

"I know. He better get well 'cause they need him. They are undefeated."

"I know, and they are headed for the state championship. It ain't this little league mess we are standing here watching now."

I almost wanted to laugh. It was really cool the parents were out there on a Saturday, supporting their kids. My parents had tons of other more important stuff. Thinking of their absence and Mr. Gunn's whereabouts made me angrier.

After the game was over, Coach came over to me as my brother gathered his things and said, "You and I need to talk."

"Coach, really, I'm fine."

"I don't think you are, young man. I haven't been completely honest with you."

"Hmm," I said. I looked at him, needing an explanation.

"I know you asked me not to have Coach Gunn around. I asked you to tell me why. When you wouldn't, I respected that decision."

"I appreciate it," I replied.

"But here is the thing, I had a hunch. You don't have to tell me if I'm right or wrong. Honestly, I don't even want to go down that road."

"What road?" I said, wondering what he knew. He wasn't a coach back then, but he was around helping out and learning the ropes.

"I guess I just wanted to tell you if you ever wanted to talk about it, I'm here. I should have done more. I should have said something, but I just missed it all. I had a little tiff with Gunn. He told me that what I saw I didn't see, but I was sure I saw what I saw. However, it was easier to take his word for it. When no one complained, I thought he'd told me the truth"

Was there any adult who had an inkling about what Gunn had done to us? I threw my hand up, grabbed my brother, and got out of there. I headed straight to the church. Not only was I supposed to drop Logan off with my dad, but I also wanted to see my father and go off on him for being pitiful in that role.

"Wait up, Landon!" my brother hollered.

I walked past Belinda, my dad's secretary. She tried to tell me not to disturb my dad, but I wasn't listening. I opened up my dad's office door. He had folks in for a meeting.

"Son, I'll be with you in just a minute," he noted, giving me a momentary glance.

"Dad, don't lie. You're never with me *any* minute. You need to do a better job at parenting, or all you love is just gonna come crumbling down on you. I'm telling you, Dad. I'm telling you."

"Son, what are you talking about?"

I turned around, walked out, and slammed the door. I wasn't even looking at where I was going. Still seeing a child's dead body lying before me everywhere I stepped had me spooked. Even the church walls could not stop my mind from thinking dark thoughts. The guilt was eating me up so much that I started running through the church. I wanted to get out in the fresh air to breathe. I bumped straight into a female. When I looked back, I saw it was Eva Blount from school. Shoot, I was bumping into her at Lockwood, and I was bumping into her at church. She looked upset too. But I couldn't deal with it. I quickly said I was sorry and headed outside for the fresh air I desperately needed to breathe.

"Folks, let's give it up as our Lockwood Lions take the field," the announcer said as the team charged into the stadium ready for battle.

Usually, I took in the crowd's noise. The screams and roars always charged me up before and during the game. If the fans were into it, then I wanted to give them a show. However, during this game, that wasn't the case. As I ran through the paper sign the cheerleaders made, I didn't have much pep in my step, and my stride was off.

I noticed Eva looking very disoriented. She was usually the sassiest cheerleader we had. I didn't want to see her upset. Thinking I was part of her woes, I went to say something nice.

"Hey, Eva. Again, I wanna apologize for continually bumping into you."

"You don't owe me an apology," she stressed.

"Running over you wasn't my intent," I said, noticing she wasn't even paying attention. "You look like your day has been worse than mine."

She shrugged her shoulder and with a slight attitude scoffed, "Okay, thanks."

I really didn't care if she accepted my apology or not. I felt bad about running into her so hard and so tough. That wasn't my style. I liked to take care of women, not bulldoze over them. However, she seemed so distracted that I didn't push. For real, of all the people in the stadium,

I understood having something heavy on your mind.

We started on defense. The big boys we were playing knocked us off the ball. Leo and Brenton were normally the dominant ones, but they were not having success stopping the run. Our opponent's running back took it to the house. We messed up our first round on special teams when the kick returner dropped the ball, fumbling it, and allowed the other team to recover the pigskin. They got the ball on their own eight yard line. They didn't even need all three tries to score again. That same power running back was on the ball again. He was built like a hog, and now he was oinking himself all the way to the end zone. Just like that, we were down 14–0. Before the half, it was more of the same.

Coach Strong got in our grills during the break. "Look, men, I'm not gonna stand here and let you guys blow this opportunity. You are fighters. You are winners. You are Lions, and you have a chance to be undefeated this season. We have a chance to have home-field advantage in the playoffs if we stay the course. We've got a chance to make it to the dome. Play like you

got something on the line. Don't give the game away. If I got one player in here who will stand up and give me heart, we got a chance. Right now all of y'all are lying down like lambs. Don't get it twisted up in here. That's not who you are. We are not cowards. We are champions. We are kings. Do I have any kings in here?"

Coach Strong always spoke my language. He was an excellent motivator. He wasn't selling BS. He cared about us.

I was a King. I was a leader. I was a champion, and I needed to start acting like it. I needed to get our team to start playing like it. The only thing going good in my life was the success of this football team, and I had to fight for that. I quit focusing on what was going on with me and started thinking about what was important to me. I was gonna win this game. Soon as it was time to go back on the field, I sprinted out there.

"C'mon, Blake, you gotta toss that ball. No more interceptions in the second half. You can do it. You the next Cam Newton." Then I looked over at the defensive leaders and said, "Brenton, force a fumble, please, top linebacker. You gotta stop their runner. He's big. He's a hog, but he can't run

through you. C'mon, wassup? You wanna look back on this game and be mad that you let him get away. And Leo, sack the QB, man. You are on your way to a school record with sacks. Amir, where are my interceptions?" And they were all looking at me like, *What you gonna do?*

As soon as I ran on to the field, Blake threw me a bomb. The ball was a little high, but I jumped up as high as I could. I caught that sucker and was ready to put my actions where my heart was. I scored.

The guys started feeding off of me. Defense had three plays, then out. I was back out there again after a great return gave us nice field position. This time Blake threw me a little dump pass. I shook off one defender, got away from two others, and scored again.

"That's what I'm talking 'bout, King. Lead this team, man. Lead this team," Coach Strong got in my face and said with emotion when I came over to the sidelines. "You are phenomenal. We're in this game, boys. Let's finish strong."

I went up and down the sidelines and said, "They're in our house. We will not be denied in

our house. Dial it up." Then I started thinking about Mr. Gunn, and I yelled, "We will not be intimidated in our house."

If I had to talk to myself to get up enough strength and courage to overcome my fears and insecurities, I was going to do what I had to do. Brenton felt my enthusiasm. He caused the force fumble and got the ball back for us. I scored another touchdown. We won.

We were not intimidated in our own house. I had to transition this way of thinking to all aspects of my life, trying to find the courage to take the next step. I quickly got dressed, ready to face what was next.

As soon as I came out of the locker room, my cell phone rang. When I opened it up, there was a video text. It was sort of faint, and I couldn't figure out who was in the seductive scene. Guys around me were cracking up, as if they were watching a great comedy.

Leo was hot mad. "Dang it, I gotta go find Ella's sister."

"What's wrong?" I asked, thinking he should be happy we'd just won a big game.

He enlarged the image on my phone. "Look at this, man. Somebody is sending around a bad video of her."

I wanted to take my phone and chuck it against the wall. It was the newest iPhone, so I wasn't going to break it. Going on and on about Eva in a defamatory way was sophomore defensive back, Colby, who'd been riding the bench since Amir came. I got really ticked.

I went off, "What the heck do you know about what you are saying?"

I guess I was hot thinking our peers were going to do the same thing with me once they heard what happened to me a long time ago. I could just see them assuming all kinds of nasty stuff. Now it was Eva, but if I talked, I'd be the topic of conversation.

Then I realized this was why Eva had been so distraught. Sure, rumors about her had been circulating for a while, but this video was on the verge of being X-rated. Now I had to let folks know that talking about somebody was wrong.

"Don't get mad at us," Colby said. "The way that guy is handling that, I want me a piece. That's all I'm saying."

I grabbed him by the collar and slammed him up against the outside of the field house. This was a girl's reputation. No one needed to trash it. I was sure she felt bad enough.

"Calm down, man. Calm down. Let him go. Let him go," Amir said to me. I wanted to pound his face for so many different reasons.

While I was angry at him, he wasn't the root of my problems. So after choking his throat, I let him go, knowing I had to figure out a way to deal with this guilt because it was getting the best of me.

"Landon, there you are. Come quick," Carlen called out from across the gate.

Right now my life just made me want to scream. I had just received the honor of the most valuable player in the game. We won, and I couldn't even enjoy it because my teammates were ticking me off with their petty ways. Carlen was bugging me, looking all spastic, like he'd been drinking coffee throughout the whole game. I just wanted to go home, get to sleep, and think of nothing. I tried putting my hands up like, *Dude, for real, leave me alone*.

Unfortunately, Carlen was following me, yelling and screaming. "It's important. Seriously, Landon, come here."

I went over to the gate and said, "Thanks, man. I know I had a good game. Appreciate it."

I guess I was an idiot because he looked at me, like, *Are you serious?* "Don't be so full of yourself," Carlen snapped.

I nodded in agreement, but he needed to hurry up. "I'm tired, man."

"I need you to go with me somewhere," Carlen said. I frowned, looking at all the players looking at the two of us.

Clearly, whatever Carlen wanted to tell me was private, and he didn't appreciate my teammates trying to eavesdrop. I wanted to yell, "Just blurt it out already," but Carlen was the kind of guy who would go off on you if you fronted on him. Why I didn't think he would try me was because I was bigger, more muscular, and stronger. But I definitely didn't want to risk a confrontation with him. He cupped his hand and motioned for me to come toward him. I sighed.

Carlen wanted me closer and yanked my collar. "Mr. Gunn is here at the game. I saw him

with two little boys. Everything ain't on the up and up. We gotta do something."

At that point, it didn't matter who was looking at me. Worrying if anyone thought there was something going on between me and Carlen was not important right now. I had my man card, and I halfway wished somebody would ask me a stupid question or try to insinuate something was going on. Truthfully, Carlen had sent shock waves up my spine with his news, and regardless of what anybody thought, I had to do something. Was this my nightmare becoming reality? No way could I let that happen.

I pointed to the end of the fence. Carlen and I both rushed to the stands. We were bent on finding Gunn.

"He's not here anymore," Carlen panicked when we got to the part of the stands where he last saw them.

"Where was he?"

"He was sitting right there in that corner with two little boys, trying to act like it was cold so he needed to keep one boy under his arm in his jacket. And I saw the boy's face cringe a couple of times. I don't trust him."

If you stood on the top of the home-side bleachers and looked behind you, you could see the parking lot. That was exactly what I did while Carlen looked down. I had to find them. Those boys' lives depended on it.

"There they are!" Carlen yelled out.

I didn't have to be told twice. I started following Carlen, and when he pointed, I saw Mr. Gunn leaving the stadium with two boys who appeared to be around Logan's age. Carlen was going too slow for me. I pushed him out of the way, but when we got down among the crowd trying to leave the stadium, we couldn't go as fast. When we got to the parking lot, we lost them again.

I turned to Carlen and said, "Which way did they go? Dang it, you were going so slow."

"I'm sorry. I'm not a wide receiver who can sprint and run the forty in four-point-three seconds," he snapped.

"How did you know that?" I looked at him.

"Watched you in PE. Amir is the only one who is faster," Carlen answered.

"No, no, no, no! I can take him," I said. My competitive nature came out.

"In your dreams."

"You know what? Let's stay on track. Where do you think they have gone?"

"When it was me, we went to his place," Carlen said.

I looked up at the moon, desperate for guidance, but all I got was the truth showing on the situation. Carlen wasn't alone. Coach Gunn had taken me to his place back then too.

It must have shown on my face because Carlen said, "You too?"

"Since he moved away and came back, he probably doesn't live where he used to."

"No, but I know where he lives now."

"How do you know that?"

"Just been casing out his place. I'm not trying to let him off the hook for what he did to me, but I did tell a couple of people, and I got laughed at. So I knew I needed evidence. I do not believe a leopard can change its spots."

"Good. My car is by the field house. Let's go find this monster," I said, all the while hoping we could catch up to Gunn before any damage was done.

When we were in the car, I had so many questions. I was feeling bad all over again, like

I had earlier in the morning. I hit the steering wheel hard. He could not hurt anyone else.

I shouted, “This is my fault. You wanted to turn him in. You wanted to say something. You wanted to get him off the streets. I’m a coward. If anything happens to those boys—”

“If anything happens to them, you’re not the one doing something to them. You’re scared, Landon, and so am I. Gunn damaged us. Nobody can blame you for how you reacted to that.”

“Don’t let me off the hook.”

When we got to Gunn’s house, it appeared to be a modest two or three bedroom ranch. While it wasn’t the same place he tortured little boys in back in the day, the layout certainly was familiar. Not even going inside, I knew there would be a bedroom close to his; one that he would have the child sleep in. He used to tell me he was gonna ask my parents if I could stay the night.

“He’s not here,” Carlen called out.

“It’s got a garage. He could be in there. How do you know he’s not home?”

“Well, there’s no light on.”

“He could be in there with one of the boys or something,” I suggested.

"No, he hasn't been parking his car in the garage. The one time I saw it open, it was so full of junk he couldn't get his car in there. He's not here," Carlen answered.

"Where do you think he's taking the boys?"

"Maybe he took them to get something to eat ... first," Carlen choked on his words. "I think he's eventually coming here like he's done before. We just need to relax, man our post, and be ready. The way he was looking at those boys, I know he intends something bad."

"Well, it was only me and him before. It was never me, somebody else, and him," I said.

"For me it was," Carlen reflected. "He let the other kid play and watch TV, and when that little boy fell asleep, he had me all to himself. Tonight I saw him favoring one boy over the other. I think that's that same setup he's planning to work with."

It was like somebody took their fingernails and ran them down a chalkboard. The thought of what Carlen was talking about was sickening and disgusting. As my blood boiled hotter than a pot of spicy chili, a car pulled up. Gunn and both boys got out of the car. He unlocked

the front door and one boy ran inside. The other looked like he didn't want to go in. When I saw Mr. Gunn grab the boy's arm and stick it near his belt, I knew I was going to have to bust the jerk. The police needed to be involved. I knew I should have opened up long ago, because at that moment, I had unthinkable guilt.

CHAPTER 5

Identical Pain

Nine-one-one, what's your emergency?" the operator asked me.

"I'm at 1213 Old National Highway. Send someone fast. A pedophile is abusing boys. He's taking them into his house. Please get somebody here quick," I begged.

Before she could ask me any questions, I hung up. My hands were shaking, my mind was racing, and my heart was about to explode. What was Gunn doing on the other side of that door?

"We've got to go in there and help those boys," I said to Carlen. "We got to bust the door down or something. We can't just wait on the police. They might get here too late."

"Let's try to look through the window. Let's try to take some pictures."

"What are you saying? Are you a pervert?" I asked. I was about ready to choke Carlen.

"No, I'm saying if we go in there before the police come, and there's nothing going on, Gunn can worm his way out of this, and we'd be in trouble for trespassing. However, if we check things out and catch him doing what we know he is—"

Frustrated, I cut Carlen off. "I'm not going to sit here and let him molest these boys. That's just not going to happen. You brought the wrong guy if you think I'm just going to let this happen to somebody else. No!"

"That's not what I mean. I'm not saying that. I'm saying almost."

"Even *almost* can make a boy have bad memories; almost letting him mess with a kid is still unacceptable," I stressed.

"We just can't go in there right now," Carlen refuted. "Don't you understand? We need proof."

Knowing he was right, I uttered, "The police better hurry up and get here then."

Both of us got out of the car and dashed across the street up to Mr. Gunn's house. We

went to the side of his house where we thought the family room might be located. Lights were on in the room shining out of two windows that Carlen and I were able to see into. Carlen looked in one, and I peered in the other. There sat one child, playing a video game and probably unaware of what was going on at the other side of the house.

"I'm going around back. You stay and keep watch on this guy," I whispered to Carlen.

When I went around back, I saw another light on. Unfortunately, even at my height, the window was too high for me to see directly inside. However, there was a trash can nearby that I turned upside down and pulled to the window. I stood on top of it and was able to see in.

I was appalled when I saw that Gunn's jeans were off; tears were coming from the boy's eyes. I could only imagine what he was planning to do next. Remembering what Carlen said, I pulled out my cell phone and started recording his criminal behavior, but then he reached for his underwear. I banged on that window so hard that I almost broke it, forgetting the unstable trash can below me. I lost my balance.

I screamed, "Carlen!"

I heard him yell, "The police are here."

Next thing I knew, I had flashlights shining in my face. Two cops surrounded me. They seemed ready to handcuff me.

Carlen yelled, "No, no! Not him. We gotta go inside. We gotta help the boys."

Once I was helped to my feet, Carlen and I, along with the two officers went back to the front of the house. Before the officer could bang on the door, Mr. Gunn came outside. He glanced at me and looked smug.

Mr. Gunn exclaimed, "What's all the commotion? What's wrong?"

"Sir, do you have some minors in your home who are not your children?" the taller officer inquired.

Mr. Gunn opened the door. "Yes, they're in here playing video games."

"And their parents know they're here?" the other officer asked.

"Of course, sir, I wouldn't kidnap any kids. We're just playing video games—"

I cut him off as memories of what I'd just seen flooded my brain. "He's lying!"

"How do you know, young man?" the taller cop asked.

"Because I saw what was going on through the window, and because he molested me when I was a boy," I stated. I was laying it all on the line.

No one moved. Gunn looked like he wanted to kill me. I stared back hard, letting him know it was on. Days ago I told him not to try me, but by getting another kid in his bedroom, he did not heed my warning. He needed to go down.

"He molested me too, officers!" Carlen yelled.

"And when was this?"

"It was five years ago for me. I know he was about to do something to one of those boys in this house," Carlen confessed.

"Boys, come here," Gunn crooned. The two boys got up and came to the door. "What were we doing?" he asked.

The one boy who Carlen watched said, "Playing video games."

The other boy said nothing. He actually held his head down. When I examined him closer, he was shaking.

"I got proof," I said, reaching for my phone.

I panicked when it wasn't there. Quickly, I patted my other pocket. Still there was no phone.

"*He's* got proof. Ask this one right here what was going on, officer," I suggested, pointing to the little guy I saw in Gunn's bedroom.

Mr. Gunn looked at the boy with a harsh glare. The boy stepped toward the inside of the house. He was scared.

I grunted, "Get Gunn away from him because he's intimidating the boy. I'm going to the back of the house, officer. Please come with me with your flashlight. Please? I've got proof."

The taller officer saw the little boy tearing up. He took the little boy to the side to question him. The shorter officer spoke into the radio attached to his shoulder and called in backup. Good, they were finally believing us.

"This is ridiculous," Gunn ranted. "I don't know what he's talking about, but I've done nothing. The boys just told you we were playing video games. Either you arrest me or you get off my property. I'm trying to mentor these young men who don't have fathers. Their moms are appreciative that I'm spending time with them. This is part of the little brother program. Ya'll may have

heard of it. I'm supposed to be with them. Molesting some kids, please! I'm a role model."

"Quiet, sir," snapped both officers.

"Officer, can we go look for my phone?" I begged.

"No. Everyone just stay still," he ordered.

Carlen yanked the flashlight from the officer's belt and ran to the back of the house.

"It's my phone," I called out so that he'd know what to look for.

I was about to run and help when the officer held my shoulder. "Don't even think about going to help him, son. Stay here."

"What's your badge number?" Mr. Gunn ordered. "I want your information. This is harassment."

It took Carlen no time to come back with the phone. He handed it to me, and immediately I was thankful for technology. I found the last video entry and played it for the cops.

"Sir, you're under arrest," the visibly appalled officer said. "Turn around!"

"It's coming from those teenagers. There is already an altered video going around Lockwood. Kids manipulate images," Gunn explained.

The cops weren't buying it. They read Gunn his rights and handcuffed him.

Another police car pulled up. Carlen and I were asked to go to the station to give a full statement. One cop car took Gunn, and the other took the boys.

As Carlen and I followed the police in my car, Carlen warned, "There's no turning back now, Landon. Everyone's going to know."

He did not have to tell me that. My life as Mr. Perfect Landon King—cool, straight, no scars—was over. Though it had been a façade for years, it was a wall that I liked up. If I had to go and do it all over again, I would tear down the wall myself to protect that boy from experiencing what I went through.

When we got to the station, Carlen said, "Gosh, seeing that video was exactly how things started for me. I was helpless, and he wanted me to do things that made me want to scream, but I couldn't because his nasty, sweaty hands were on my mouth."

"Well, we helped that boy," I acknowledged. I was able to relate to the nightmares Carlen spoke of.

"Yeah, we did," Carlen said. "We helped that boy, and that is what is important."

"Are you okay?" I asked the little boy when we all met up at the police station.

"Thank you for saving me," he said. "You're Logan's big brother. I'm Andrew, and your brother and I are in the same class. You can call me Drew. Thanks for helping me."

I was shocked the boy knew me. The little guy knew my brother. I was astonished and relieved that things weren't worse.

The boy continued, "I didn't know what he was going to do. He was scaring me, asking me to do stuff that was wrong. He held my mouth, and he told me he was going to show me something that I would want to—"

I told Drew that it would be okay. Gunn's *m.o.* had not changed. I was glad I listened to Carlen and let things get as far as they could without endangering the child. We did need something on tape as hard evidence. There was no way I wanted Gunn to intimidate this boy into keeping quiet like he did to me years back. There was no way I wanted him to be able to weasel out of his

hideous act. There was no way I wanted him to feel like what he was doing was right. Though I was raised that it was wrong to wish the devil on anybody, I hoped he burned.

About an hour later, after everyone was questioned, we were told we had to wait for our parents in one of the interrogation rooms. Carlen and I were relieved to know that Gunn was being booked on child molestation and endangerment charges.

"I want my mommy," Andrew cried.

I was not a girl. I did not feel comfortable holding him. To be nurturing was not in my DNA. Carlen got up and patted his back.

Carlen soothed, "It's going to be okay."

Carlen's response did not seem to be settling him enough. It was like Drew wanted me to tell him it was going to be all right. Because I knew Gunn was going to be locked up, I told the little boy things were going to be all right. When the interrogation door opened and another police officer entered, all four of us stood at attention. It actually felt like we were being locked up, like we were the animals who had done something wrong, but when we were escorted out front, we

saw why we were hidden away. There were news cameras, and other policemen were escorting them out of the building.

A swarm of officers shielded us all, especially the youngsters. But I could still hear questions hurled in our direction by several exiting reporters. “Did Gunn hurt you guys? Do you know of other boys who have been attacked? Why haven’t you said something before?”

There was question after question after question. I realized this was going to get around school fast, but I did not know it was going to be a media circus.

After the front was clear of the media, Drew called out, “Mommy!”

He rushed over to his mom. She gave him the comfort he needed. That warmed my heart.

They walked over to me and she said, “Hi, I’m Ms. Wells, Drew’s mom. The officer explained everything that happened, and I can’t thank you enough for saving my son. You put yourself on the line. You’re a famous high school football player with a famous father. Thank you.”

The other little boy was with his mother. She was greatly appreciative, and she thanked

Carlen as well. Carlen seemed to have no problem in accepting their gratitude. It was killing me, though. Those boys should not have even been in that situation. I should have done something when the jerk first entered back into my life. Carlen even told me he had seen him around younger kids. I knew he was hanging around at the park. I kept thinking about if the worst had happened. I shook my head and bolted away.

"We want you to wait on your mother," an officer declared.

I wanted to tell him that I was not a kid, but the kid in me longed for my mother too. She needed to hear from the cops all that had happened to me. She needed to know my struggle. I wanted her to understand all that I'd been carrying around for so long. When I saw her come through the precinct doors with her eyes filled with tears, I knew she felt as sad as I did. She immediately rushed to my side.

"You know?" I sobbed. She just hugged me tightly and apologized over and over again.

"Yes, they told me everything on the phone. How could I not know what this man had done to

you? Landon, please forgive me, son. I'm so sorry. He better be glad he's in custody because I just want to rip his eyes out," my mom raged. I saw an unfamiliar side to my normally calm mother, but I knew exactly where her rage was coming from.

Where Gunn was concerned, she and I had similar thoughts. Seeing her fire, I realized we were a lot alike. Since we didn't spend much time together, I didn't know that.

"And you saved a little boy by coming clean. I know it's got to be hard for you. You're a man now. They said we can go out the back and avoid these reporters. Son, why didn't you tell me?" she asked.

I pulled away, not wanting to be her little man at that moment. Those days had gone by. A part of me was still real salty with her. I shrugged my shoulders, not having a legitimate reason why I did not open up.

"I should've known," she admitted.

"He was at Logan's football practices."

"Are you serious?" she roared.

"Yeah, but I think Coach Brown knew something too, and he banned Mr. Gunn from coming over there." I looked her eye to eye and grabbed

both her of hands. "Mom, you have got to promise me something."

"What, baby, what? I need to tell your father this right away."

"Okay, well, you gotta promise me two things," I said, knowing I wanted to speak to my dad about this.

"Talk to me, Landon," she soothed.

"As bad as you feel for not being there for me," I said, looking directly at her, "you got to be there for Logan more, Mom. Go to his games. Ask him how his day went. Don't just trust him to anyone. Yeah, you gotta save the world, but make sure you save your son. It seems like yesterday, you always say, that I was in fifth grade. Mom, a year and a half and I'm gone. Spend that time with Logan so you have no regrets, please."

She could not hold back the tears at that moment. They just spilled from her eyes. My heart was aching too, but I did hate seeing her cry.

"And, Mom, please don't say anything to Dad. I just want to break this in my own way."

"I understand," she promised. "I can't believe this, Landon. He molested you. I hope he burns." My mother shook her head wearily.

What happened to me was evil, but being in my mom's arms felt good. Having her finally know the truth about this horrible incident gave me the strength to begin the healing process. I felt more like me than I had in years.

"This is the last place I want to be," I thought to myself. I was sitting in my dad's office at Lakeside Baptist Church on Sunday morning instead of being at the service listening to his sermon.

My mom made me get up and come to church. We didn't sit together in service, though. So when she went to take her seat in the front pew, I stayed behind in the office. I'd only made it home hours earlier, and though I didn't get much rest, I wasn't tired. I was overwhelmed. The story was in the news. Though my name wasn't yet mentioned, it was only a matter of time. I was still seventeen and a minor. The papers weren't allowed to print my name, or so I understood. Still, I was very upset. I walked to the smaller sanctuary for a quiet place to think. I needed a higher power to help me because I felt too down to be uplifted on my own.

I went through the door and sat in one of the pews. Unable to hold back the pain of my past, I started sobbing. The tears would not stop.

Needing answers, I yelled, "Why? Why did this have to happen? I was too little to fight back. Why weren't *You* there for me? Why wasn't my dad there either? No one sheltered me from the guy, and now I got to deal with this."

I paused, as I thought I heard movement. When I heard nothing more, I figured it was a rodent. I made a mental note to talk to my dad about getting the church sprayed.

Dealing with bigger problems, I continued, "Why was I molested?"

"Wait a minute! *What!?*" I heard a girl's voice shout out.

"Who is in here?" I demanded. I could not believe my privacy had been violated in the safest place imaginable.

"Forgive me … I'm so sorry," the girl, whose voice I recognized, said.

I dashed to the back of the small room. I needed to know if I was correct in my assumption of who it was. I was very surprised that I was right. Eva Blount was in there.

"It's *you*?!" I blurted out in a voice that was irritated and perplexed at the same time. "What are you doing here, Eva?"

She came toward me, and I saw compassion in her eyes. She was very different from the tough person I'd encountered over the last week. Eva had always been known as the sassy, feisty one, but now we were two peas in a pod. Both of us had devastating things that we were dealing with. The whole school knew her turmoil. She was the star of a sex tape, and everyone we knew had seen it. Now she knew my secret.

When she got close to the door at the back of the room, she did not leave. Instead, she stood close and said, "You know my story. Everybody does. I came in here to pray or vent or something, but I wasn't moved until I heard you."

"I can't believe you were listening in," I said, looking away.

She turned me back toward her and scolded, "I mean, you just walked in here, and you didn't ask if there was anybody else inside. Keeping it real, this was my space before it was yours."

I realized I needed to chill. "All right, calm down. I'm not saying you shouldn't be in here. I

just wish you would've said something before I started spilling my guts. I don't want anybody to know, dang."

"I get you. Not sure exactly what happened, but it's your business. I apologize for not letting you know I was in here, but something awful happened to me as well. I don't just mean the tape everyone has seen. Something far worse, Landon. I'm just not the same since it happened, and I'm on edge," Eva confessed, backing up.

"You can't sleep?" I asked, connecting with her pain.

"Nor eat," Eva replied.

"Or relax."

"Yeah," she cried.

I stepped closer and wiped her face. "You wanna talk?"

"Maybe," she said, wanting to open up.

"I feel ya," I croaked. My tears began again, though I tried hard to fight them off.

She stepped closer this time. She wiped my face. I felt embarrassed, but her touch made me feel better. It was weird.

We decided to open up to each other. I was not prepared for what Eva shared. I thought I

knew what she was upset about. However, it was not only that a video was floating around and her rep was ruined. No, she was devastated because she was raped. The guy recorded his horrible actions and made her feel violated all over again.

"Eva, it is tough to hear that such a terrible thing was done to you."

She clutched her heart. It was like she cared that I cared. We had the same plight. Maybe I was led to this small sanctuary to find a friend.

Eva began, "I went out on a date with the guy who made the video. He wanted to take things further, but I said no. Somehow he made the recording look like I wanted it, but it was fixed. Why this happened to me I'll never know, but it woke me up. I am now taking life seriously."

"I get you," I agreed. "The substitute teacher we got in math was my little league football coach. He did so much extra with me. He took me to games, bought me ice cream after practice, and was like a dad to me. My real dad was so busy building this place that he was grateful I had a male role model. He spoke so highly of Mr. Gunn that I never told my parents what happened. I was so traumatized by what happened

to me in the fifth grade that I never played middle school ball."

When I told her all that I felt comfortable enough to share with her, she reached out and took hold of my hand. That touch gave me weird strength. She understood what I was going through. We had both been sullied. We had both been wronged. We both had identical pain.

CHAPTER 6

Fixed Mistakes

We needed a change of scenery. The solemn church atmosphere was not working for us. We didn't want to hear my dad's message. So I suggested we go get something to eat. I wanted to keep connecting with her.

"You didn't have to get me breakfast," Eva said as we ate at the Waffle House next to the church.

"After I bit your head off, I owe you," I said, taking in her beauty.

I was stunned when she put her hand on mine—stunned in a good way. Instinctively, I smiled and reached for her other hand. Our eyes didn't move from one another for a long while.

Finally, Eva pulled away and said, "I'm happy we connected."

"Yeah, who knew you were Dr. Eva," I said, making her smile.

"It had to be hard seeing Mr. Gunn after all those years," she commented.

"Too much. It's been a nightmare seeing him at school, seeing him around my brother, seeing him practically molest another child."

"You're right. My mom was babbling this morning about something like that on the news. I didn't think it affected anyone I knew."

Shaking my head, I said, "Shoot, I didn't want this out. People gonna think I'm gay. It ain't like I got a steady girl."

I wanted to take back those prejudiced words. I could not believe I was opening up to Eva this way. She was so easy to talk to.

Surprising me again with a dope response, she said, "I feel ya. People saw the video of me and made all kinds of assumptions. People think they know me and assume—"

"You're loose," I blurted out.

I waited for her to go off on me. She ate some food and kept her cool. Guess she knew we both

had questionable reputations. I did wonder why she liked dating college dudes.

"Why don't you give guys your own age a chance to win your heart?" I wondered.

She huffed, "Because y'all are so immature."

"Oh, so you're dissing me now," I pouted.

She smiled, "Well, maybe some of you have grown up."

We locked on one another again. I'd never thought of Eva the way I was thinking of her at that moment. She was everything I'd want in a girl if I was looking. She was gorgeous, sassy, and real. And I learned she was vulnerable. That hard shell was all a front. I felt like she needed me in her life. And as long as I felt that was the case, I would be there. Not that I had extra time. However, for her I knew I'd make the time.

"So how do we fix our lives?" she asked.

"I need to tell my dad. This is all over the news, and I want him to hear it from me. Not sure how he'll take it. I wish that I didn't care, but I do."

"Preaching to the choir on that one. I'm in the same boat. My dad hates me, and that's eating me up inside."

Feeling protective of her already, I said, "What's he tripping about? He just got married. I saw you that day standing up for him."

I could tell she was surprised I saw her. While I had my own issues that day, I did think she looked fine in her gown. Maybe that's why when I saw her down before the game, I wanted to lift her up. Maybe I'd been drawn to her over the last couple of weeks and never realized we were connecting or that she was moving me.

We were doing so well connecting. Then she turned somber all over again. Guess her dad really had her down. Or maybe it was the rape. It could be that I was annoying her. Shoot, I could not figure out why she pulled back and looked away.

I turned her face to meet mine. "I don't know what you're thinking about, but you know you didn't bring any of this on yourself, right? You get the right to say no."

"Obviously not."

"No! Obviously, he crossed the line, and he needs to pay. Do your parents know?"

"Only my mom."

"What about the police?"

She laughed. I stood stern, waiting on her to explain as none of this was funny to me. She nodded and began talking to me.

Eva said, "I didn't go to the police at first. So when I did, the cops said I had no claim."

"That's bull!"

"My dad's an attorney, so I think if I talk to him—"

"You've got to talk to him."

As we got up to leave, she took my hand and said, "Let's go tell our dads together. Deal?"

"You'd go with me?" I asked, relieved that I would have a partner to lean my shoulder on.

"We can see each other through it."

"Cool," I said. We agreed she'd go tell her mom, who was attending services, and then she would meet me in my dad's office.

When I reached the pastor's offices, I realized it wasn't going to be easy getting his attention. So many people followed him up to his space after services. I could look on the faces of folks and tell they needed him desperately. I was about to walk out, letting other folks have my dad.

My mom walked through his office corridor. She would not let me exit. I tried to tell her other

people needed Dad. She hugged me tight and told me this time everyone else was going to wait.

"Baby, you've been patient enough," she encouraged. "Do you need me to go in with you?"

Kissing her cheek in thanks, I said, "No, ma'am."

"Okay, I'll be down the hall in my office if you need me. Logan is in there waiting for me. We're going to watch his game tape from last week," she chuckled.

Before she left, she told my father's armor bearers that I needed time with my dad right away. I was motioned in. Before they could shut the door to give us privacy, I spotted Eva.

"Let her through," I ordered to everyone wondering what she was there for. "She's with me."

Eva smiled with relief that I spotted her. I told her thanks for coming up to help. We sat in the chairs in front of my dad's desk.

"Landon, you know I've got to preach in Savannah this evening. Your mom texted and told me this was important. What's going on?" he asked. He sat behind his huge mahogany desk, which would have been intimidating except for his warm tone.

"Dad, meet my friend Eva," I said. I was bummed that he was busy moving papers and not giving us his full attention.

"Hello, Miss Eva. Forgive me," my dad said.

"Hello, sir. Nice to meet you. Landon just has me here for support," she said with grace. "Your son has been through something terrible. He needs you to listen."

At that moment, my dad's world stood still. For me to bring a girl he didn't know into his office to help me tell him something heavy worried him. I told him everything. We were all uncomfortable, but oddly, Eva's presence made it all more bearable. My dad heard me out, and I could tell he was beyond hurt.

"I'm not going anywhere. This has to be dealt with," my dad roared.

"Dad, you need to preach," I lamented. I was overwhelmed that he'd put off a prior commitment for me. "Besides, I need to go help Eva with something. We can talk more later."

Dad was so somber. "I am sorry, son. I should have kept you safe back then. I am stunned and humbled. You and your brother mean everything to me. I have not been the father that you needed."

I was thankful that we connected. He cared. For the first time, I felt my dad wanted to be a good father to me, protect me from harm, and bring down the one who wronged me. Though he didn't want to keep his plans, we agreed it was for the best. He thanked Eva, and we headed out to see her dad.

Eva and I were full of hope when we went to see her father. After all, my encounter went so well that we had no reason to think hers would go otherwise. However, her reveal to her father went awry. He wasn't home, and when she spoke to him on the phone, he didn't believe her story.

After she hung up, she said, "He accused me of making the whole thing up to get attention. I admit I didn't want him to get married. We were getting close, and I did not want distractions. I gave the newlyweds drama. But, Landon, I am devastated that he wouldn't believe me. What am I going to do?"

"Eva, don't sweat it. He'll come around. Everything will be okay. We'll get you through this. I'm here," I said with little confidence.

I meant every word, but I could barely stand myself. My issues had me so weak; I was frail.

Eva knew it. She wasn't buying the hope I was trying to sell her. When we got to her house, she got out of the car and slammed the door. I wanted to go after her and make her know all would be well, but I couldn't fix the world. So I let her be.

The school week was brutal. Everywhere I went I heard people talking about my situation. I heard: "That was the boy who got raped," and "He probably never told anybody because he really liked it," and "He's the one who saved the little boys." Comments went from good to bad. Nobody confronted me directly, so I chalked up their talk to just that, talk. As long as I stayed strong, their words wouldn't affect me.

However, as much as I tried telling myself it didn't bother me, their words cut to my inner core. I was irritable. I had insomnia. I was depressed. If it wasn't for being able to talk to Eva, someone I really felt understood how it was to deal with all this, I probably would not have been able to survive. She also had to deal with people talking about her and making accusations.

I made a mental note not to be judgmental again. I remembered trying to be the cool one

during freshman year, making jokes about fat people. I cracked on poor kids, nerdy kids, and the ones who weren't as smart as me. If they weren't a jock, they weren't safe.

While I quickly got over that immaturity sophomore year, it now resonated with my new experience of being a victim. My behavior back then was really wrong. I didn't *ever* need to do that again. Folks had feelings, and people needed to not make people feel horrible.

Thankfully, football practice leading up to our next Friday game was also a saving grace. I wasn't as brutal in practice, wanting to tear folks' heads off or smash them to pieces or anything, but I was intense. I wasn't concentrating in the classroom, but I was focusing on the football field. I hoped the vicious game could fix me and numb the pain. I suppressed those feelings for so long, but over the last couple of weeks, they had come gushing out to flood my world. This whole situation of folks mouthing off about me was unacceptable and out of my control. I wasn't ready for my teammates to turn on me and talk about me like I wasn't there. It was time for us to play ball and win our next game.

I caught Waxton saying, "If King turns soft on me ..."

"I know, but just calm down," Blake told him almost cosigning.

Hearing that exchange hit me hard. Blake didn't stand up for me and say, "You don't have to worry about that. Landon is cool. Why you trippin?" Nothing! He did not try to squash the drama. That really upset me. Brenton and Amir were talking to each other.

"I just wished we would have known, man," Brenton said. "He was my teammate. I should have been there."

When Leo walked into the conversation, he said, "Dude, I been thinking the same thing, man. Shoot, Coach Gunn knew not to try me."

Leo said that like I was some weak punk. Like I looked like somebody ripe for the picking and that's why Gunn chose me. Like I had done something wrong and deserved all this. It was too much to hear them pity me.

However, Leo continued feeling sorry for me and said, "He just don't seem like the same person. I don't know if he's aware of it. He's jumpy, edgy. It's like he's on crack or something."

"If I didn't know him," Amir offered. "I'd say he was going through withdrawal."

"Well, we gotta help a brother out," Leo said. "I don't even know if he can play tonight. Seems like any minute he'll explode like a bomb."

"Why wait for the game?" I yelled at the three of them. "Why don't I explode right now?"

I grabbed somebody's helmet from the benches and threw it across the locker room. There were a couple of chairs, which I kicked over one at a time. A teammate was drinking a cup of water and I upended it, making its contents spill all over.

"Hey, hey, settle down, man," Leo rushed to me and said.

"You better step off. You're the one talking all that junk. You wanna fix me? Let me give you something to fix." I shoved him hard.

Coach Strong stormed in, "What the heck is wrong with you, King? Come on, we need to talk. The rest of you guys get out there and warm up with the other coaches."

I walked away from him and banged on the lockers. I wanted to take my head and bang it instead, but I just repeatedly used my fist.

"Settle down, son. Get a grip."

"C'mon, Coach, don't play me. Don't act like you don't know what's been going on around here with me. It's a huge scandal, and I'm caught dead in the middle of it."

"But you're still standing. You're a survivor, man," Coach said while he studied me. "When I was younger, my dad used to beat me to a pulp. Folks used to say he was a strict disciplinarian. I know some of my ways I get from him, but I try every day of my life to break the cycle of the cruelty and not pass it on to Blake or my daughter."

"The past is supposed to make you stronger; now everybody thinks I need to be fixed," I said.

"Son, you don't need to worry about what other people think you need. It's time to dig deep down inside yourself and figure out what you want. How do you want to live? What do you wanna focus on? Do you wanna stay bitter? Or do you wanna become better? Make no mistake about it, you are a hero. You saved those kids."

"Please! I should have spoken up long before."

"And that's why you can't even see the good because you're so full of what you didn't do. Man, look at that glass half full. C'mon, if you hadn't

said anything, who knows what would have happened? Be proud of yourself."

He patted me on the back, and as we were going out of the locker room, I was amazed at the sight before me. My dad was standing there. He looked like he desperately wanted to speak to me.

"Coach, can I speak to my son for a second?" my dad asked.

I cried out, "Dad, what are you doing here?"

"There's no place I'd rather be. I've noticed the media attention. Even though you are a minor and no names have been released, people suspect it was you, and they are coming down hard on me as a parent. And rightfully so. I should have known what was going on with my own son. But that's not why I am here. I owe you an apology, Landon. I wanted to tell you that I'm with you every step of the way as this criminal is prosecuted." Then he placed his hands on my shoulder pads and said, "Look, I don't want you to think any of this was your fault."

"Why did he pick me, Dad?"

"I don't know, son. But we trusted him. If you blame anyone, blame us. You can't blame

yourself," my dad reasoned. "We'll talk about this so much more, Landon. But I hear that my son has skills. You just get on out there and put on a show. I came to see for myself. Wassup?"

"Got you, Dad," I said, giving him dap. Then in a serious tone I said, "Dad, thanks for coming."

Soon as I jogged on the field to warm up, Leo, Brenton, Amir, and Blake headed my way. Leo said, "I'm sorry, man. We didn't mean to make you feel like we were putting you down."

"You know you our boy, right?" Blake asked.

"I just wanted folks to hush up. I just wanted to defend you more," Amir said. "I didn't want you to feel like I didn't care. You've always been upbeat. Don't lose your joy, man, for real, for real. Now can we go win this game?" he shouted.

"For sure," I responded. Shaking hands with them and giving them dap during our cool high-fives, let me know deep down that I was still me, strong Landon King with heart and courage. No one could take that away unless I gave it away.

We were at an away game. We were playing our rival, Mays High School. Mays had a

dynamic football team. However, we were ready to win. I was ready to play.

Our team dominated the game. We were rolling in every facet of the game. Brenton, Leo, and Amir were holding them scoreless. Special teams was doing their thing not letting the other team get yards after the catch. The field position game was won by us. Offense was popping too. Waxton was running all over the Mays players. Blake and I connected for two nice touchdowns as well.

We scored three touchdowns, but Brick could not kick the ball through the uprights for the extra points. So we won, 18–3. My teammates were surrounding ER. Everyone was hoping he'd be cleared to play soon. We certainly knew in the playoffs that we'd need him.

When I exited the locker room, my dad rushed over to me. "Son, you are so good. I'm proud of you. You're a very good player. *Very* good. Enjoy your teammates, and I'll see you later."

On the ride back to Lockwood, I was deep in thought. I knew the grand jury would be making a decision about Gunn's fate soon. He could not walk. This had to go to trial. I knew he would not

accept a deal from the DA because he was too cocky and felt he'd done nothing wrong. He had to be crazy. However, I hoped that would not be his defense if this went to trial.

When we got off the bus, I looked for Eva. I hadn't seen her the entire game, and I wanted to make sure she was holding up. I wanted to call her, but I didn't want to be pushy. I wanted to ask her if it was okay if we kept in touch. But I could not find her. So I went over to her sister with my boy.

I asked, "Have you seen Eva?"

Ella searched around, "She was on my bus, but she got off first when we pulled in the school."

Whitney, a senior and co-captain of the cheer squad, heard us talking about Eva and walked over. "I saw her head to the stadium. Thought she was gonna meet a guy or something."

Ella said in a panic, "It's so dark over there. Why did she go there? She was quiet the entire game. Something's wrong."

Knowing she was still a basket case, I said, "I'm going to go find her."

"Ella and I will come too," Leo insisted. I nodded, and the three of us headed to the bleachers.

When we got to the stands, Leo took Ella and they looked further down the stands. I searched in the darkness, hoping for enough light that I'd see movement. I had to find Eva. She needed help getting out of her pit of gloom. She had wallowed for far too long.

Sure enough, when her sister and Leo called her, I saw glistening come from what appeared to be a necklace. She wasn't moving toward the voices; she was fleeing. She backed up, and I touched her shoulder before she hit a steel beam.

Eva was so tense that I startled her. She jumped. When she saw it was me, she let out a sigh of relief.

In a caring tone, I said, "Hey, you. What's up? You got us all worried."

Obviously happy it was me, she rested her head on my chest. "This is too much. I'm sick of hurting. I was such a resilient person before this, Landon. Now I feel so weak and fragile. What people say bothers me. I even detest myself. I see no end to the despair."

She tried to walk away, but I held her closer. "Getting all this out is the first step. I meant it when I said that I'm here for you."

"How can you help me when you're going through so much?"

"Let's continue helping each other," I offered.

She paused and then pulled herself away from me. "I don't want everybody knowing about this," she said. "Your boy is helping Ella find me. Did you tell him my business?"

I knew she was upset. I always needed her to know I would not betray her. If she just calmed down, she would see she could make it. I knew. I'd been there.

"I haven't told him a thing. Check with your sister. Relax. Leo is cool, and he cares about your sister a lot. If he knows something, he won't share it."

"Just great," she vented.

Feeling she was overwhelmed, I said, "Come on. Let's just get out of the stadium. You're gonna be okay. I'm going to see to it."

"I'm tired. You just don't get it," Eva cried.

Though she was exhausted, it was clear she wanted relief. She took my hand, and we walked to the lights. Feeling her clutching my hand, I knew I would honor my word. I would make certain she smiled again.

"Here you go, pretty lady. We're at the back in the parking lot," I whispered. She had her head nestled on my shoulder.

Eva peered up at me with her lovely mocha eyes and said, "Thank you for caring. You really saved me tonight."

"Oh, don't go giving me all that credit."

"If the shoe fits, you must wear it well and not be modest. Now I have your number."

Hoping that was a good thing, I asked, "Huh?"

"I know chivalry is deep within you. Leo isn't the only one who has turned in his playa card," Eva teased, showing me her mood was lighter.

Without even realizing it, I kissed her brow. Both of us stood for a second. She was as shocked by the gesture as I was. Then she smiled. I mimicked her movement. As I watched her flee into her sister's arms for comfort, I felt better. Eva was safe. She had hope. Though I could not change what happened to either of us, I was determined that we would revel in salvaging all the good that we could as we fixed mistakes.

CHAPTER 7

Just Verdict

For the first time in a long time, I was starting to appreciate myself again. Being able to help Eva actually helped me. We were victims, but we could still be victorious. Though a lot of this hurt, the pain was only making us stronger. Another first for me was sitting in my *father's* church and watching my *dad* preach. I watched him with adoration. Unlike many Sundays gone by, where I looked up to the man in the pulpit like he was more than us, I saw the person for who he was.

Pastors were supposed to be there. They were supposed to care. They were supposed to give comfort. I hadn't had my dad do any of those

things until now. Now, the way he supported me and rallied around me helped me to move on. His caring allowed me to open up. I was able to see he had been giving a gift to his parishioners. Watching him, I understood how many loved and respected him.

When it came to my faith, I wasn't really certain what I believed. I had been baptized. I said the right things, and I knew a lot in the Bible. Honestly though, I hadn't truly decided if I was going to follow a higher power in my life. A part of me resented the church because my dad spent so much time there.

It felt as refreshing as a cool drink after a long day's practice when I heard him speak. My ears were open to truly hearing the message he gave, and it spoke to me deep down at the root of my soul. His words stirred me emotionally.

Pastor King preached, "So, I know life is hard. You guys know I know this because my own family has been through a trial recently. We often ask ourselves, why did this happen? Why did that happen? And it bothers us when things come our way and turn our world upside down. It sets us on a spiral because we did nothing

wrong. However, worse happened to the Man who we came here to worship. He died for things He didn't do. He died for me and you. So, while you might have a broken heart and are falling apart, know that He was innocent of any crime, yet He was still crucified. He had to go through that all alone. Now, brothers and sisters, here's the great thing: He gave His very life for you and for me. So, hold on, brother! Hold on, sister! You *can* get through the hardship. Because He died, we can face tomorrow. If He didn't hang, then we wouldn't have hope. You are still here for a reason, and He won't put more on you than you can bear. Be encouraged. He's got you."

That was a lot to take in, but I got it all. At the end of the sermon, I had no doubts anymore. Being a believer was something I claimed because I was a preacher's kid. Now, my faith truly was a part of me. I had strength all along. Gunn did not take it. He beat it down, but he did not beat it out of me.

I needed that strength too, because the next day I was testifying before the grand jury. I took deep breaths and told myself I could do this. Even though Gunn hated me, I wasn't going to let him

shake my confidence. Regardless of what was decided, I was telling all I knew.

"In your own words, could you explain to the grand jury what happened to you long ago when the defendant was your football coach?" the prosecutor asked.

I began, "Coach Gunn was someone I trusted. Someone who I thought had my best interests in mind. He was very friendly with all of us kids, but I remember him telling me that I had special skills ... that he wanted to help me hone my attributes. I believed that he wanted to make me an even better football player."

I went on and told the whole story. While I was strong, I could see people's eyes filling with tears. How an adult could take advantage of a child was despicable, but that's what happened to me. A huge weight felt lifted when I told the grand jury every gory detail. I could imagine Mr. Gunn smirking at me like I was lying if this were a trial. However, neither he nor his defense attorney was allowed to be in the grand jury room.

"Thank you for your testimony, young man," the prosecutor concluded.

Be Real

I saw the defense lawyer sn
courthouse, but he was not allow
appear before the grand jury. The
some sleek-looking dude in a loud su
imagine his voice asking me, "So, it's b all
these years, and you haven't said a thing. We're supposed to believe that you remember all this in such detail? You can recall everything that happened when you were in elementary school? Nothing you sketched?"

But none of those questions were asked because I was under the protection of the grand jury. Shoot, Gunn hadn't even been charged yet. That's why we were here. The grand jury wanted to make sure that there was enough evidence to charge him.

Before I knew it, my testimony was over, and it was Carlen's turn. I was not allowed to stay in the room.

When he came out, I asked him, "Did you stand strong?"

"Man, I told them what happened. I could never forget what happened. We were little. He took advantage of us. He needs to be behind bars."

"Well, hopefully he will be. This is the first step. I owe you an apology, man," I said to Carlen

"Why?"

" 'Cause I judged you."

"It's cool, man. I know y'all football players get a little homophobe."

"Well, that ain't right."

As Carlen and I went on to predict whether or not justice would be served, I just had to take a deep breath and step back from it all. I decided that I could only do what I did: stand. But if Gunn got back on the streets, I wouldn't be responsible for my actions. Therefore, they better send this to trial so I wouldn't end up in jail for taking justice into my own hands.

It was interesting being in an assembly with all the males in my school—interesting because the assembly was about inappropriate contact. Our principal, Dr. Sapp, was a cool dude and real forward thinking. With two intense scandals hitting our school at the same time, he put the girls in the auditorium and the fellas were in the gym. There were so many eyes roaming my way. I had to deal with it because it was what it was.

On the panel there was a male physician, who looked so old that folks around me were saying there was no way he even knew his own name. There was a police officer, who I actually remembered from Mr. Gunn's house, and there was a psychiatrist, who looked like a nerd. Those were the three panelists.

Everyone was shocked when the old doc got up and said, "Y'all better keep them johnsons of yours in your pants. I'm not here to preach abstinence, but for real, for real, it is the only way to ensure safety."

The old doctor had swagger. He was quoting facts about boys and STDs. I was stunned to learn that every day eight thousand teenage boys in the United States became infected by a sexually transmitted disease.

Then the cop said, "And not only can you get in trouble physically when you have improper contact, but if you force yourself on a lady or gentleman, that's rape, folks. And don't drink, guys. The legal age is twenty-one. None of you here are that old. Seventy-five percent of the men involved in date rape had been drinking or taking drugs before the attack happened. Additionally, one out

of six boys are sexually abused before they reach sixteen years of age."

"And the biggest thing we wanted to talk to you about," the psychiatrist said, "is the emotional scars, depression, and instability that comes from unwanted encounters. We want you to know that as young men, you should be leaders. If a young lady says no, that means no. If someone has done something to you, then you need to talk about it with your parents, another family member, a teacher, someone, anyone—"

"Please, that stuff ain't going on here," somebody called out from across the gym. People started coughing and laughing. I saw some folks pointing in my direction. Someone even shouted out Carlen's name.

"Oh, that's right, my bad," the same voice from across the gym yelled out.

Tired of folks, I just stood and yelled, "Can I have the floor?"

Dr. Sapp acknowledged me. I nodded my head in thanks. A microphone got passed to me. I laid it all out there.

"I'm not enjoying being the brunt of the little jokes around here. Don't think I haven't heard

some of the stuff that's been said about me. Some saying because I was molested, now I'm a fag. Don't stand too close to him or he'll turn you into a vampire. He tries to act all tough to overcompensate because he's really a weak wimp. You can say whatever you want to say to me.

"For the longest time, fear of those comments kept my mouth shut. Here's what I know now, and I sure wish I could go back and change things. If there's anybody else in this school who's dealing with sexual violence, you're not alone. You'll feel better if you talk to somebody. These folks up here are keeping it real for us. Those laughing, leave. If it ain't about you, then good. However, I know now that there are some brothers hurting, and if you don't address that, then your pain can hurt more people," I lectured, not holding back one thing.

"Landon, I know that wasn't easy, but thank you," Dr. Sapp offered.

I was surprised as people started clapping. I didn't need anyone to applaud. I just needed to get through to people who might need help.

"I just want to close on this note," Dr. Sapp said. "That was bold of Landon to share. Here's

the thing: my door is open anytime to discuss what you need to, man to man. If I don't have the answer, I'll pull whatever resources necessary to talk about what we need to. No one needs to be intimidated. You're young men, stand up and be accountable. Members of the panel are going to stay up here for another hour. If you'd like to talk, don't feel like you need to rush to your next class. If you don't need to, head straight to your class because we're voting for the homecoming court. Hey, guys, remember you're young and you should enjoy life. Don't carry any unnecessary burdens, and don't mess up yourself by messing up someone else's life. Be smart! Know that you've only got one life, which you should live to the fullest."

As he dismissed us, I saw several guys go up to the podium. I was so surprised that my words spoke to so many. I did not know if they wanted to hurt somebody or if they'd been hurt themselves. But they wanted to talk. They wanted to get help. They wanted to get counsel. Our school *had* to get better because of the session.

As I was headed out of the door, Dr. Sapp stopped me and said, "I'm proud of you, Landon,

for getting all of those guys in line to talk. That took courage."

"I just hope it helps folks."

Pointing to those talking to the panelists, he said, "It is and it will."

I went on to class. I ran into Eva. She and I had our last period together. Turns out she shared in her session as well. Coming clean took a lot out of both of us. I really dug the fact that we were in the same place. With the dance coming up, I stayed bold and asked her to accompany me. A smile crossed her gorgeous face when she answered yes. To make her day even better, she was announced the junior class representative on the homecoming court. I'd be escorting a princess—to me she was just that. The fire Eva had walked through had redefined her. Now her classmates had spoken; she was a gem.

The prosecution was finishing up its case to the grand jury. Carlen and I felt compelled to be present in the courthouse. I so hoped everything would stick. When I got there, I heard a friendly familiar voice.

"Landon, over here," ER hollered. "Dad, this is Landon King. Landon, I want you to meet my father."

"Hey, young man, I've been watching you play. You're an outstanding wide receiver," ER's dad said.

He sort of looked like a redneck, but he shook my hand real strong and smiled my way. Having him tell me he liked my ballin' was cool. I had to start learning that you could not judge a book by its cover.

"Son, I'll be right back," his dad said. "I'm going to grab the last few books of paperwork."

"What's going on?"

"He's overjoyed. Finally, I'm eligible!"

"Stop it, man," I said. The two of us did our little football dance in the hallway of the courthouse.

The tight-dressing professional lawyers were looking at us. ER did not have great rhythm, but he was an all-right dude. He had taken a lot of smack for not being able to get out there and kick for us. Going into the homestretch, we'd have him; every aspect of our football team's game would be topnotch.

"You told Coach yet?" I wondered.

"No, just found out. You're the first person who knows. This is cool, right?" ER asked.

Trying to get an understanding, I said, "I don't even understand what all the issues were. You live with your dad."

"Yeah, but my mom has legal custody, and she didn't really didn't want me to move. My coach from Grovehill ratted me out. It just was weird. They made me go through a few extra hoops, but that's behind me. What are you doing up here?"

"Going to find out if *that man* is getting charged," I said. I dropped my head, unable to fully articulate my frustration and angst.

"It's going to be all right," he encouraged.

"You're right. I just don't know what I'm going to do if they set him free and don't take this thing to trial."

I sat on a nearby bench. While I could not control the outcome, the weight of it was affecting me greatly. ER sat beside me. No words were spoken. Just having him park himself beside me really moved me. It showed that he cared, and I would never forget him for that. I'd have

his back on the field—for sure! Stone giving me hope tightened my respect for him. I could tell he wanted to talk. I looked his way so that he knew I was open to hearing what he had to say.

"You believe, right?" he asked, pointing to the cross necklace I usually wore for style.

I nodded. "Go call Coach, man. You know he's going to be psyched."

"I just appreciated your support," ER commented. "You always had my back. I know I haven't really said much all season. I've been sort of in my own little world. I just want you to know I appreciate you."

"That's what's up," I said to him.

"Dude, good luck. See you at practice." Then ER was off.

I sat outside the grand jury waiting room. I did not want to enter. My phone buzzed with an incoming text from Eva.

She wrote, "Can you talk?"

I texted back, "Calling now."

"If you are busy, I can wait."

"For you I got a sec," I wrote.

When I sent that last text, I was stunned by my own admission to her. I was really taken

with the lovely chocolate sweetie. My boys had been tripping over the Lions cheerleaders. At first, I didn't think they were all that, but now I knew firsthand that they were fly and fierce. I really wanted to make time for Eva. This was a new feeling, and I wasn't scared of all my emotions brewing over her.

I dialed her number, and I enjoyed hearing her sweet voice.

"Hey," she said. "I just want to really thank you. Asking me to the dance, helping me deal with my pain when you're going through your own … really cool. I don't let people in, but you showed me maybe I need to start."

"Look, can I give you a call after I leave out of here?"

"Sure, and it's gonna be all good, you know? No worries."

"Hmm, now look who's helping who," I flirted.

"That's the least I can do, right?"

"Thanks," I whispered.

When I opened the door to the waiting room, I was shocked at the sight before me. The room was packed with people. Carlen waved me over to him. There were tons of young guys

in there with their parents. There had to be twelve or more.

"What is going on?" I said to Carlen.

"All these boys have been testifying because *we* stood up and said what happened to us. When it hit the news, a lot of them told what happened too. We made people feel like it was okay to report Gunn."

"Wow," I whispered.

"One of the kids told me that Gunn was taking him for ice cream, but they didn't go to the ice cream shop. Gunn said he had some at his house, and there was no need to buy it. The boy thought it was okay until he was eating his ice cream, and Gunn had to use the bathroom. Gunn came out in his towel and ... well, he told him that he had ice cream on his mouth. You can imagine what happened next," Carlen recounted with a frown.

Gosh, I did not want to hear any more. I was shocked when I turned around to get a better look at who was in the waiting room. I saw Waxton, the starting running back on our team. Carlen then told me that Wax gave testimony that was extremely graphic and very heart

wrenching. I don't know how Carlen knew this, and I didn't want to know.

I did not realize that my parents were in the grand jury waiting room. I had driven on my own after I had worked out. They both came up to me and hugged me really tight. I then went over to Waxton, and we gave each other a five.

"Everybody doesn't need to know this, right?" Wax said to me, letting me know he wasn't as strong as he always let on.

"What happens in the courtroom stays in the courtroom as far as I'm concerned, bro," I said to him. We connected on a deep level.

"Yeah, thanks, man," he nodded. "I should've stood up. I should've said something. I should've done more."

"The point is that you are doing it now, man. It's all good," I preached. We gave each other dap.

The prosecutor stepped out of the grand jury room and made an announcement. He told the waiting families that Gunn would be charged on many counts of child abuse, possessing child pornography, sexual assault, and the list continued. It looked like there was a lot of strong evidence to lock him up for a long time.

"He's going down," Carlen sighed. He hugged his mother.

Walking out of the courthouse with my parents, I reflected that for so long I had suppressed all that Coach Gunn had put me through. He had taken my youth. He had stolen my innocence. He had weakened my spirit.

Now, I felt renewed. It was like I seeing the world with new eyes. I had peace with my father. I had found being a playa wasn't half as satisfying as opening your heart to a lady. Most of all, I had made peace with myself. What was done to me was not my fault. I was a victim, but I still had power and swag. I wasn't going to be victimized.

Being real, life was definitely hard sometimes. I realized that people had issues, but you could not let your problem become someone else's problem. You had to man up and admit that you might need help. You had to be true by being honest and truthful to yourself, by lending a hand, by caring for others sometimes more than you cared for yourself, and by not letting people take advantage. Be bold and don't care

what others think of you. Know it is okay to get help if you need it. Yeah, this was a real good day. If there was any fairness in the world, Gunn would be going away for a long time. So many young boys deserved justice. The healing could begin with this just verdict.

STEPHANIE PERRY MOORE is the author of many YA inspirational fiction titles, including the *Payton Skky* series, the *Laurel Shadrach* series, the *Perry Skky Jr.* series, the *Yasmin Peace* series, the *Faith Thomas Novelzine* series, the *Carmen Browne* series, the *Morgan Love* series, and the *Beta Gamma Pi* series. Mrs. Moore speaks with young people across the country, encouraging them to achieve every attainable dream. She currently lives in the greater Atlanta area with her husband, Derrick, and their three children. Visit her website at www.stephanieperrymoore.com.

DERRICK MOORE is a former NFL running back and currently the developmental coach for the Georgia Institute of Technology. He is also the author of *The Great Adventure* and *It's Possible: Turning Your Dreams into Reality*. Mr. Moore is a motivational speaker and shares with audiences everywhere how to climb the mountain in their lives and not stop until they have reached the top. He and his wife, Stephanie, have co-authored the *Alec London* series. Visit his website at www.derrickmoorespeaking.com.

WANT A DIFFERENT

point of view?

JUST *flip* THE BOOK!